CAPE WRATH
and
THE HELLION

CAPE WRATH
And
THE HELLION

Paul Finch

First Published in 2002 by
Telos Publishing, 5A Church Road, Shortlands,
Bromley, Kent BR2 0HP, UK

This edition published in 2015 by Telos Moonrise:
Dark Endeavours (An imprint of Telos Publishing)

Cape Wrath © 2002, 2015 Paul Finch
The Hellion © 2015 Paul Finch

ISBN: 978-1-84583-903-1

Cover Art © Martin Baines
Cover Design: David J Howe

The moral right of the author has been asserted.

British Library Cataloguing in Publication Data. A catalogue record for this book is available from the British Library.

This book is sold subject to the condition that it shall not by way of trade or otherwise, be lent, resold, hired out or otherwise circulated without the publisher's prior written consent in any form of binding or cover other than that in which it is published and without a similar condition including this condition being imposed on the subsequent purchaser.

CAPE WRATH

Then came Ivar, Great Ivar, also called 'Slayer' and 'Boneless'. Ivar, destined to add the crown of York to his crown of Dublin, but also to bring great murder and pillage to all the lands of the English.

The son of Ragnar, who was flung to Aella's adders, Ivar brought vengeance on all the Christian kings of Britain. Three of them he gave up in heathen rites. Their hearthmen he laid waste in bloody battle, their fair women he raped and enslaved and fed to his crews like meat to the dogs.

Ivar of the berserk rages, also called 'shape-shifter', 'wolf-spirit', and seer, it was said, with the single eye of Odin. His conquests and devastations ran like fire through England, 'til only the kingdom of Wessex held against him. This too he might have had, but White Olaf, Ivar's brother-in-arms, crossed the wide sea to Norway, and Ivar went unto the lands of the Gaels, already burned and sacked by him, yet ripe now for more.

Boneless Ivar was the terror of this age.

Monastic Chronicle of the Farnes, 870 AD

ᛗᛏᛗ

'Oh, shiiiit!' Craig cried, jumping to his feet, setting the boat rocking wildly. 'Check it out!'

'You great Welsh prat!' Barry Wood shouted, grabbing hold of Linda to protect her.

Craig ignored him, and pointed skywards. 'A sea-eagle, look!'

'Big deal,' Barry replied.

'What's so special about a sea-eagle?' David asked.

Craig shook his head. 'You peasants. It's one of the rarest birds in Britain. It even went extinct at one time …'

Alan leaned back against the gunwales and stared up, finding he could just about distinguish an aerial form lofting about one of the higher coastal crags.

Craig meanwhile felt at the pocket of his cagoule, where his camera was always kept handy. 'I'd love to get a couple of shots of it while we're here.'

'I'm sure we'll find the time, Craig darling,' came a soft but authoritative voice from the aft section of the outboard. Everyone looked round. It was Professor Mercy, who even bundled up like all the rest in a sweater and oilskins, looked as alluringly feminine as ever. Her flaxen hair hung in strands from under her woolly hat. 'Now sit down, hey. The sea around the

Stair is supposed to be dangerous enough without you trying to capsize us as well.'

Craig sat, but his attention was still focussed on the distant shape of the eagle. 'I'll bet it's eyrie's up there somewhere. You want to see the places they nest. Talk about precarious.'

Alan couldn't help wondering how precarious their own position currently was out here in the middle of the firth; the rough water beneath them was so deep it was inky black. Then there was the island, Craeghatir; on a map it was nothing more than a tiny spot off the tip of Cape Wrath, mainland Britain's northern-most point, but in reality it was very different. He turned and viewed the awesome mass of rock looming towards them over the whitecaps. The sea seemed to boil around its feet. From deep, deep below it there rose a dull thunder, like the boom of cracking stones.

ᛏᛈᛞ

The Stair was easily as impressive as McEndry, the doughty old boatman, had said it would be, but docking there was a perilous procedure.

It was basically a narrow canyon, with a strip of gravel beach at its seaward end. Farther in, the beach was buried under jumbled heaps of boulders, the debris from some landslide way back in geological time, and it was this that afforded passage up and onto the island, which from the ocean appeared as a natural fortress of soaring limestone cliffs, utterly impregnable.

Even at the Stair – the only point on the entire circumference of the isle where explorers might get safely ashore – a boat had first to negotiate all manner of obstacles, rocks both visible and submerged, a terrifying swell and backwash, and closer in, explosions of surf, where the breakers, having charged full strength into the gorge, were funnelled violently together and detonated with elemental fury. With each impact, there was a phenomenal suck and crash of pebbles, the echoes of which rolled and rolled in the chasms of the cliffs.

The passengers hung on for dear life as McEndry clung to his tiller and stoically guided them into the cleft. The outboard – at first glance a sturdy 12-footer – now felt flimsy indeed. It was tossed and thrown from side to side. Spume spattered everyone, ice-cold brine slopped over the gunwales. It didn't surprise Alan at all that no-one had settled on Craeghatir in living memory; that in fact, aside from the infamous megalith, the only sign of man on this island was the lighthouse on its north-westerly tip. That was the way it was likely to stay if the only way to get ashore was via this roller-coaster ride.

He glanced overhead as they sailed in. The sliver of pale blue sky bore a crisscrossing pattern of seabirds. Their harsh cries rang down, and were amplified in the canyon, which made them sound strange and unnatural. It reminded Alan of the other reasons people were supposed to have avoided this place; the reasons none of them had really discussed yet, thinking perhaps they were too adult to entertain such fancies. Alan certainly thought that *he* was too adult, but that didn't prevent the discomfort he felt just to recall some of the ancient stories told about Craeghatir.

Then McEndry cut the engine. They were still several yards from the beach, but he lifted his propeller, leaped out of the back of the boat and began to push. Now they understood why he'd come out wearing his plastic 'factory-ship' dungarees. A moment later, they'd crunched onto the shingle and were able to climb out, though even then they didn't feel shielded from the fury of the sea. The waves were rumbling at incredible volume, the air was filled with spray; for all his waterproof packaging, Alan found himself drenched through. He turned to Nigel 'Nug' Unsworth, who was busy buckling his rucksack back over his oilskins.

'Tell me, Nug: why do I always fetch up in places

like this?' Alan shouted. 'This time last year, I was in the Black Wood of Rannoch in pissing rain, searching for Celtic artifacts, of which we found zilch; the year before that, I was on Bridestones Moor, freezing my knackers off digging up some really exciting relics of medieval charcoal-burning. And now look. A lovely day in the middle of summer, and instead of toasting on the Costa del Sol, supping sangria and checking out the tan-lines, I'm here with you lot.'

Nug grinned. With his sturdy frame, long hair and untrimmed moustache and beard, he visibly resembled a Viking, which was quite appropriate on this particular expedition.

'Nah, you wouldn't appreciate summer on a sun-lounger, man,' he laughed. 'Watching the babes wiggle past in their thongs when you could be out here rubbing ointment on your blisters, checking your arms and legs for tick-bites.'

'Just up Alan's street that,' said Barry Wood, shouldering his way past. 'He cracks on that he finds this tough going, but really he lives for pain. Wears a pair of leather undies, with metal studs in the crotch. Thinks no-one knows.'

Alan gave Nug a patient look as Barry lumbered away to where Linda stood shaking water from her plastic coverall. 'I'm sure I'm going to have a good time up here,' he said quietly, 'I'm just wondering at which point *he's* going to die and make it perfect.'

Nug slapped him on the shoulder. 'You never know. Strange things happen in wild places. And Britain doesn't get much wilder than this.'

McEndry, meanwhile, who'd made this trip once already today with his son, had now pulled the boat up fully onto the beach, then approached Professor Mercy, who was standing talking to Clive Tilley, her second-in-command. McEndry was a raw, red-faced fellow, and his hair blew about his head in a scraggy grey mop. If anyone looked like a native of this part of the world, it was the boatman, though curiously, like many of the north Highland Scots, his accent wasn't particularly strong.

'Your gear's further up,' he said, indicating the heaped rocks at the far end of the canyon. 'Me and Angus took it up there for safety. Tides are a funny thing on Cape Wrath.' He considered for a moment, then turned to face the rest of the team. ' Don't any of you come down here unless you have to, especially when there's a heavy sea running. Think this is bad, think again. It isn't. We get real high water up here.' He gazed at the mountainous seas beyond the cleft. 'You get washed out there, you've no chance. No chance at all.'

'Thanks for the advice,' Professor Mercy said, taking a wad of polythene-wrapped £10 notes from her anorak pocket and handing them over to him. 'But they're a pretty sensible bunch, for students. I hand-picked them, myself.'

McEndry nodded his thanks as he pushed the money under his dungarees. 'They'll need to be. Craeghatir isn't like anywhere they'll ever have been before.'

'They're a hardy lot too,' Clive assured him. 'We took all this stuff into consideration when we chose them.'

'Aye, maybe. Well …' and the Scot moved back towards his boat, 'I'll be back on Thursday on the six o'clock tide, with the supplies you ordered. You've got your phone and everything?'

The Professor nodded and patted the waterproof

satchel at her side, which contained the satellite telephone. 'A couple of us have got mobiles too, just in case.'

Again the boatman pointed out to sea. Six miles away, the smudge of the Scottish mainland was just visible over the blue rollers. 'Coast Guard station at Durness will pick up a distress call,' he said. 'Better make sure it's an emergency, though. They'll not be pleased if you turn 'em out because you've run low on baked beans or something.'

Professor Mercy, who'd made about a hundred other hazardous field-trips during her career, simply smiled.

On the whole, Alan mused, she was right to be confident they could handle the hardships of the island. They were a more-than-reliable crew. All volunteers of course, as any field-trip over holiday time would require them to be, but specifically chosen even then, firstly because they got high grades and were original thinkers – 'fresh minds for fresh finds', as she was fond of saying – and also because they were physically robust, which was essential on an outdoors dig. In this respect, only David Thorson had a question-mark against him. At 19, he was the youngest present, and still in the first year of his bachelor's degree. On top of this, he was short, plump rather than fit, and though amusing and good company to be with, of uncertain temperament when the going got tough. Even now, as they yomped their way up the high rocky stairway, Alan watched David struggling, sweat pumping from his fat, freckled brow ... and this was without any kind of kit to carry. Alan knew that Professor Mercy had included the lad because his father was Assistant-Treasurer back at the college, but he still wasn't certain it was a good idea.

Of course, it was no easy climb for any of them. It was hazardously steep for one thing, while many of the rocks were loose and shifted alarmingly beneath their booted feet. Here and there, there were patches of green bladderwrack – proof of McEndry's assertion that sometimes the seas off Cape Wrath ran very high indeed – and these proved slippery and treacherous.

Alan turned, and found Linda coming up behind him. She was a pert, lithe creature, whose love of aerobics and martial arts kept her in terrific shape, though even *she* was panting and puffing, and generally having trouble on the loose surface.

'Okay?' he asked, stopping as she came alongside him.

Linda gave him a disdainful look. 'Course I am.'

'Hey … I only asked. I *am* allowed to show concern, I suppose?'

She sniffed. 'Bit late for that, don't you think.' And then she pressed on up.

Alan gazed regretfully after her. She these days effected a 'pageboy' look, keeping her chestnut hair in a fashionable bob. Though most of it was currently stuffed under her anorak hood, it went with her lovely green eyes to near perfection. Which only served to pain him more.

For several moments, he watched her from behind as she scrambled away up the Stair. Then Barry appeared alongside him. The burly athlete didn't say a word, but made a point of giving Alan a deeply suspicious once-over as he passed. Alan ignored it, shook his head at the unfairness of life, then continued with the ascent.

Within 10 minutes or so, they'd reached half way, where, as the boatman had promised, their various haversacks and sealed packs of rations were awaiting them on a flat shelf. As they loaded up, Alan glanced back down. Far below, framed in the mouth of the gorge, he saw McEndry chugging his way back across the firth. Higher up here, away from the windy seafront, the sun was noticeably warmer. Alan unzipped his oilskin coat and loosened the thick fleece beneath it, remembering dozens of TV commercials on which the highlands and islands of Scotland were portrayed in their finest summer livery; an unspoiled paradise of heather-clad mountains, verdant pinewoods and blue tidal inlets.

And at first glance, inner Craeghatir appeared to live up to that holiday-maker's dream.

They came up over the top of the Stair in their ones and twos, but invariably, each one of them then stopped short to take in the stunning scenery, for what seemed like the entirety of the island lay spread out before them. It was basically a plateau, about three miles across but concave, the lower central portion dipping down into a sweeping glen, with a blaze of lush green mosses and white fluffy cotton-grass at its far end, indicating peat bogs. Higher up, on the glen's sloping sides, deep stands of Scots pine dominated, probably the haunt of rare birds like the osprey and crossbill. Only in the island's high south-western corner, did the trees thin out and the bare hillside take over, veering sharply upwards into sheer Alpine crags that towered several hundred feet above everything else.

'Fancy going up there to find your sea-eagle?' Nug said to Craig, as they processed inland.

The bird-spotter grinned. 'Going to have to. It won't be coming down to us.'

'You sure it's what you think it is?' Alan asked him.

Craig nodded eagerly. 'The sea-eagle's highly distinctive. Got a snow-white tail and big square wings. Nothing even comes close to resembling it, not even the golden eagle. I'll tell you, it's a rare sighting for a British ornithologist.'

Serene moments passed as they strolled down into the glen, the sighing of the sea falling gradually behind them, the sounds of insects taking over. As the ground levelled out, the dry, rocky soil of the upper slopes slowly softened, and soon they were ploughing through knee-deep clumps of bilberry, the early season berries only just starting to redden. The heather grew thick and springy under their feet, and was now laced with sundew and asphodel. As often as not, it concealed broken sticks and loose, greasy stones, which made the going progressively more arduous. On top of this, the heat grew steadily. At last Professor Mercy stopped and unslung her backpack.

'Climate control, folks,' she announced.

They halted thankfully, broke out a few bottles of water, then began to strip off their waterproofs and sweaters, and pack them away. As they did, Alan glanced up and spied, framed between two distant hillsides, the glass compartment of the lighthouse's lantern-gallery. The station was unmanned of course, as so many were these days, and, as far as he knew, located at the end of a spit of land jutting out from Craeghatir's most north-westerly point. He'd seen many lighthouses before, but it never ceased to amaze him how they always had the opposite effect from the one you'd expect. Instead of reassuring you that civilisation wasn't so far away after all, they usually served to reinforce the unnerving impression that, yes!, you really *were* on some far-flung outpost in the very back of beyond, a long way from the nearest ambulance and even further from the nearest pub.

And appropriately, from that moment on, the island seemed to possess the aura of a place untouched by time. Once the lighthouse had slipped out of view again, there wasn't a trace of mankind; no litter, no habitation, no tracks or paths of any sort. Down at the base of the central depression, which was perhaps 70 to 80 feet lower than its outer cliff-tops, the soggy peat gave way to deep, clear pools, which the explorers had to circumnavigate. The air around these was alive with midges; there was also a drone of bees – clearly there'd be honeycombs somewhere close at hand. To either side, the pine trees closed in, but as always in true Caledonian woodland, the spaces between them were vast and airy, the floor-ways lying knee-deep in undisturbed drifts of fallen needles. Aside from the bees, there was a still, tranquil silence.

The archaeologists moved in straggling single-file, but Clive and the professor strolled ahead, savouring every new moment. In their many years working in the faculty, they'd been together on field-trips all over the British Isles, and, perhaps in true kindred-spirit fashion, had at length become lovers. This was an unspoken fact of life back on campus, though few would openly acknowledge it for fear that it might reflect on the twosome in professional terms, not that those who didn't know them would automatically believe it. At first glance, Clive wasn't the sort of bloke you'd expect to win a woman like Professor Mercy. He was big and ungainly, and, with a constant sleepy grin on his face, looked disarmingly like a teddy bear. But, as all his students knew, he had hidden depths. As well as possessing a nice, easy-going character, he was a good conversationalist, had an infectious sense of humour and knew his subject inside-out. He was also, like the woman in his life, completely at home in the great outdoors. What Clive didn't know about the basic lore of the British countryside wasn't worth knowing.

'Very different from the Western Isles, isn't it,' he commented, as they roamed along. 'The Western Isles are generally treeless. Soil's too poor, rocks too porous.'

'This place is a natural bowl,' Professor Mercy replied. 'Even though it's limestone, the rainfall gathers, keeps everything well-watered.'

Slightly behind them on the path, David Thorson had observed much the same thing.

'Funny no-one's ever settled on it,' he commented.

'Well they did, didn't they,' Craig put in. 'Speaking of which ... I wonder whereabouts *that* cave actually is?'

'I was wondering when someone was going to mention that,' Alan said.

Craig shrugged. 'Well ... it's only a story, of course. There might not even be a cave.'

David was interested, however. 'What're you guys on about?' he asked.

'Nothing,' Craig replied with a grin. 'It's bugging Alan.'

Alan turned and gave him a look. 'Tell him, if you want. Doesn't bother me if he ends up shitting bricks afterwards.'

Craig sniggered, so Nug took up the story: 'In 1115, some Irish monks tried to settle here, but according to the chronicle they didn't last a month.'

'Why?' David asked.

'We've only got their word for it, of course, but apparently they went home again telling stories about strange noises ... snuffles, snarls. They even wrote that the devil left his claw-marks on the door to their hermitage.'

David gave this some thought as they plodded along. 'Probably just that there weren't any altar boys to shag,' he finally said.

'Very cynical for someone so young, David,' Alan replied.

'Well it's a crock, isn't it?'

'I sincerely hope so,' Craig said.

David didn't say anything else, and a few minutes later he'd stridden off ahead, catching up with Clive and the Professor.

Alan shook his head. 'Told you he'd end up crapping himself. He probably hasn't even camped before, apart from in his mum's back-garden.'

'I'm sure he'll have his uses,' Craig replied.

Alan nodded. 'Oh yeah. He'll ensure we get the funding to come back again in August.'

Nug hooted with laughter. 'Now who's being a cynic?'

ᛏᚼᚱᛖᛖ

The cave-mouth was a dank black aperture under thick tufts of mat-grass. As an entrance-way, it was roughly triangular, about seven feet by eight feet at its highest and widest points. Nothing stirred inside it, but a smell of earth, roots and damp, decaying leaf-rubble exhaled from its deep and hidden recesses. It could have been any cave-mouth had it not been for the crude mark of a cross, scored on the high stone lintel.

'They actually lived *here*?' said Alan, with a shiver.

Beside him, Nug gazed with fascination into the dripping depths. 'In winter they'd probably need the shelter. I don't suppose they had much choice.'

Alan glanced around. 'I wonder what happened to this door the devil supposedly left scratches on?'

'Give us a break, man. It was 900 years ago. Probably turned to dust by now.'

That of course made sense, though standing as they now were, confronting hard evidence that at least part of the legend about Craeghatir was true, it was hard not to wonder if other stories were as well. Joseph Sizergh, a mariner ship-wrecked here in 1798, had never been rescued alive. His diary was found floating in the sea by a fishing-boat. For the most part, the bloodied, water-logged pages had been unreadable, though enough was gleaned from them to divert the boat to Craeghatir, where he appeared to have endured several months of 'ungodly horrors'. A search was duly mounted for the castaway, but in vain. No trace of Sizergh was ever found. The modern theory held that, driven mad by desolation, he'd finally attempted the perilous six-mile swim to the Scottish mainland, and inevitably, had failed; though others wondered if something more sinister than loneliness had been the cause of his suicidal bid to escape.

Since then, mainly from the days when the lighthouse was manned, other weird stories had emerged; concerning unfamiliar runes cut into tree-trunks, and curious items – bones, shells, dead seabirds and the like – found set out in bizarre but deliberate patterns. At least one lighthouse keeper had lost his mind on Craeghatir, throwing himself from the lantern-gallery, while another had reported a dirge of odd howls, wolf-like in tone.

'I wonder if this cave goes to any depth?' Alan finally said.

Nug shrugged. 'Can't go too far, can it. I mean, we're on an island.'

Alan mused on this. 'Well … only one way to find out.' And he switched on his torch.

Light stabbed forwards, at first showing only the dirt floor and its rubble of dead leaves and dried pine-needles, though gradually the other dimensions of the cave became visible. The twosome pressed into it. The walls were of stippled limestone and dripping with moisture. Tangles of roots and rank vegetation hung down from above. There was a rich loamy smell, tainted slightly by decay. Beneath their feet, the forest-type rubbish petered out and soon they were walking on stones and hard-packed earth.

'How far are we going in?' Nug asked.

'Dunno,' Alan mumbled. 'I thought it would've stopped before now.'

And then, abruptly, they came to the back of the cave. The ceiling sloped down with such suddenness, that Alan almost cracked his head on it. He stopped sharp and shone the light around ... to find a complete dead-end.

'This seems to be it,' he said. 'Good, let's go back ...'

Nug sniggered. 'Hang about. We've got to check for hidden doors first; secret passages.'

Humouring him, Alan roved the torchlight over every possible nook and cranny. 'Doesn't do any harm to check, I suppose.'

'Better check what you're standing in, too,' Nug added. 'This is probably the part of the cave those monks used as a crapper.'

Alan looked slowly round at him. 'Nice.'

His buddy shrugged. 'Hey, there wasn't much hygiene back in ...'

Then he sensed the presence. They both did. The sudden, unexpected presence of a figure standing directly behind them, silent and still in the darkness.

'What the ...'

Both turned violently round, fists clenched and ready.

But it was only Linda. Regarding them critically.

'*Jesus, Linda!*' Alan snapped. 'You *crept* up!'

'No I didn't,' she replied. 'I walked.'

'Hmm.' Nug glanced around at the low ceiling and damp walls. 'Poor acoustics in here, probably.'

Linda appraised them both by the light of the torch

... and found them wanting. 'Fearless fellas, eh? I'm really impressed,' she said after a moment. 'Anyway, assuming you two haven't discovered anything interesting – the idea of which was a bit of a laugh in itself in my opinion – the Prof wants you at the camp.' She turned and set off back.

Rather awkwardly, the men followed.

'Why?' Nug asked her as they emerged into daylight. 'Something come up?'

'Mission briefing, apparently,' she said. 'The Prof wants to make sure we're all singing from the same song-sheet.'

From the cave mouth, they walked back together, carefully picking their way around the 200 yards or so of bog and pool, until they'd reached the first cover of the trees, where the rest of the party had pitched their tents and were now starting a small cooking-fire. They had opted to bivouac here, at the western end of the glen, because it was well protected from rainfall by the spreading boughs of mature pines, was close to fresh water though in itself located on higher, dryer ground, and at the same time sheltered by the island's inner north-western slope from the perishing, often wringing-wet Atlantic winds ... but also because Professor Mercy had spotted the monks' former hermitage, and suspected that this place might well be 'the historic heart of the island', as she put it. As experienced outdoors folk, they'd each of them brought a single tent, all made from nylon and double-skinned, which helped reduce condensation within and was proof against insect infiltration. They'd erected them in a circle around the space cleared for the fire, but not too close to it, for obvious reasons.

Alan was pleased to see that Linda had placed hers

on the other side of the camp-fire from Barry's, and couldn't resist commenting on this as they strolled back together. 'Glad you've only brought a one-man tent,' he said confidentially.

She stopped and looked round at him. 'And what would it matter to you if I'd brought a two-man?'

'Well, it might be a bit distracting. All that noise at night.'

She gave him a withering look, then started walking again. 'Don't be pathetic, Alan. It doesn't suit you.'

'Me, pathetic?' he said, irritated. 'What about you? Shacked up with that Charles Atlas wannabe, just to make a point!'

'I'm not shacked up with anyone,' she replied heatedly.

'Does *he* know that?'

'It's none of your business, is it!'

Detecting an atmosphere, Nug had walked ahead, but the warring duo were almost back among the tents now, so they had to lower their voices anyway. Even then, Alan didn't feel he could let it go. 'What do you mean, 'none of my business'? Jesus, Linda! Didn't we have something good going?'

'You're the one who played away,' the girl retorted.

'A sodding one-off!' he hissed. 'At a party, when I was totally pissed.'

They were now within earshot of the others, several of whom had looked curiously round.

'Let's just drop it,' Linda said, flustered. 'Enough people here know about it, without us embarrassing them all to death again.'

This time Alan bit his tongue. She was right. Another scene in public would not help in any way. He stood back, hands in his pockets, and watched helplessly as his former girlfriend went straight over to Barry's tent. The big guy had just come out of it, and now put an arm around her shoulder as Professor Mercy called them all to attention.

Not for the first time, Alan wondered how he'd managed to lose a babe like Linda; more to the point, how he'd ever managed to lose her to someone like Barry Wood. The big lunk might have been the best number-eight in the college rugby union club, but he was a crude, hard-edged sort. His blonde hair and good looks belied the aggressive, loutish persona beneath. Alan couldn't work out whether Linda had fallen in with such a shallow jerk simply because she was on the rebound, or through some deep insecurity on her part. Was she, for example, one of those desperate young women who need always to be adored come fair weather or foul? Or was she simply trying to get at *him*, openly punishing his infidelity by parading round with one of those he regarded as a lesser mortal.

Then again, Alan wondered – with his usual lack of self-confidence – what made *him* so special? He wasn't a bad looking kid for 26, he supposed – dark haired, dark eyed, reasonable physique through years of self-imposed PT – but he'd never exactly been a lady-killer. Pairing up with Linda had been the highlight of his love-life thus far ... but it wasn't as though he'd *deserved* it. He certainly hadn't been able to offer her any more than many of the other guys at college. Perhaps he should write the whole experience off as a hard lesson?; for a brief time, he'd got lucky – very lucky – and now that luck had run out.

And all because of a stupid one-night stand.

He shook his head ruefully. It wasn't as if he even specialised in one-night stands; he had lost his virginity at 18, but even before Linda had come along, his assignations had been few and far between. If only he'd been ...

'We're not boring you, are we, Alan?' said Professor Mercy.

Alan looked up, startled.

Everyone was watching him. They'd formed a group at the far end of the camp about ten yards away, and were now seated on the ground. The Professor, standing in their midst, had evidently been about to let forth when she'd suddenly noticed him off in a world of his own.

He hurried to join them, mumbling an apology and something about having been up since the crack. The Professor, as was her way, nodded patiently, waited for him to find a place and arrange himself comfortably there, then continued: 'Now ... I think we all know what we're doing. I'm sure four months of intricate planning won't have slipped any of us by. But let's just refresh ...'

And she did.

In the quick, concise but oh so compelling fashion that she, as Redditch University's leading medieval historian and archaeologist, had made her speciality. In vivid fashion, she recounted the known facts about the object of their mission; Ivar Ragnarsson, also called 'Ivar the Boneless', an earl of the much-feared Danish clan Lothbrok, and probably the most famous Viking of his or any other age.

'As well as satisfying the traditional Viking image of looter, slaver, pirate, mass-killer on a terrifying scale, Ivar was also a military genius, without doubt the most successful Norse warlord of the ninth century,' the Professor reminded them. 'After his father's execution in the adder-pit at York, he launched a five year vengeance raid on Britain, in that time devastating vast areas of England, Ireland and the Scottish Isles. His ferocity terrorised even his own followers. Of course, he was reputed to be *berserkir* – a warrior possessed by the wolf-spirit, whose madness carried him past all pain and reason in the heat of battle, and whose victims were deemed direct offerings to the all-powerful entities that were the Norse gods.'

As always, Alan found it difficult not to be awed by his project-leader and personal tutor. Her combination of brains, knowledge and beauty was almost mystical. It seemed utterly appropriate that her expertise should centre on the so-called 'Dark Ages', that half-forgotten era between the fall of Rome and the rise of medieval Europe, when fact interwove with myth, and 'civilisation' meant the power of petty lords dependent entirely on the spears of their hearth-men and the wiles of their 'wizards'.

'But in what way was he 'Boneless'?' David Thorson asked. 'Not very flattering, is it?'

'They reckon it was because he was really agile,' said Barry. 'You know, could jump over spears and shield-walls and such.'

Alan snorted: 'You got that out of a movie.'

Barry shrugged his big shoulders, as if it didn't matter to him that much, which when he was close to Linda, nothing really did.

'No-one knows for sure,' Nug cut in. 'Just one of the many mysteries that surround Ivar.'

'Perhaps it meant he wasn't fully human?' Craig mused. 'Like he was a spirit creature, or something. You know, had an astral self.'

'Well he *was* supposed to be a sorcerer as well as a

war-chief,' Alan conceded.

'Course ... you've heard one outrageous theory,' Linda chirped up mischievously. 'That he was gay.'

Instantly, there were snorts of derision.

'A theory formulated in the Sixties no doubt,' said Barry, as always stung by references to anything non-hetero.

'No,' she argued. 'The story is that he was called 'Boneless' by his brothers, when he was young, because he couldn't get it up for the girls. The nickname just stuck.'

'So how come he ended up having sons?' Alan wondered.

'Well that doesn't mean anything,' she retorted. 'Look at Barrymore. He's got kids.'

There were more sniggers, more expressions of disbelief.

'No, but it's unlikely,' Clive put in. 'Being gay was frowned on but accepted by most pre-medieval civilisations, but the Nordics weren't one of them. It's true that their society was based on male-bonding, but to them, any man who couldn't satisfy a woman was the scum of the earth – a failure, a total weakling.' He turned to Linda. 'If your theory's true, it's impossible to see how Ivar could have risen to the prominence he did.'

There were more mutters about this, more arguments, until the Professor cleared her throat noisily. 'As fascinating a subject as Ivar's sexuality might be, do you folks mind if we just concentrate on what's important for the moment? And on what we're doing here.'

The group fell quiet again, and Professor Mercy resumed her lecture. She recalled how Ivar had died in

Ireland some time in 873, but that no-one knew where or how. She then went on to the ancient Irish chronicles, recently uncovered and translated by a colleague of her's at Cork University. Excitingly, those chronicles had described how 'a tyrant called Inguar' had been laid to rest on 'the island known as Crae'. This almost certainly meant Craeghatir; more to the point 'Inguar' was a common Gaelic pronunciation of the Danish name 'Ivar'. A resulting, rather tentative investigation had gone ahead and had quickly uncovered a previously unknown barrow located close to the single stone megalith for which the island was renowned, but horrendous winter weather had brought the mission to a premature end. Now, with summer finally here, and the permission of the Highlands Heritage Board secured in writing, a fuller expedition was being mounted. It was in Professor Mercy and her team's remit to carry out the first phase, excavating the barrow and its surrounding area.

'I think it's fascinating,' she concluded, 'and a great, great honour, that we … *nobodies*, let's be honest … could be among the very first people in 11 centuries to set eyes upon Ivar the Boneless. Remember how mysteriously his life ended. A figure of fury, a colossus of carnage, who cast as black a shadow in the west as Attila had done in the east, simply dropped from history. We know a little bit about it, of course. After nearly a decade of depredations, he turned away from the British mainland for monetary purposes. Knowing that his chief ally, Olaf the White, was by then bound for Norway to press his own dynastic interests, Ivar had intended to make himself sole controller of the Irish Sea trade-routes, and already with a vast haul of slaves and booty to divide as spoils among those who would welcome him in the Emerald Isle, it seemed he couldn't fail. But despite that, he did. The Danes were defeated in Ireland, and Ivar promptly vanished from the records. Literally vanished.

'Only to reappear now ... and here.'

There was a momentary silence.

Here, they each of them thought. *Craeghatir* ... a rugged, desolate isle just off the storm-ravaged point of Cape Wrath. A lost place; a forgotten place. In the words of Joseph Sizergh: 'A savage, awful isle, all stones and shells and the bones of ancient beasts; to maroon a man here would be worse than to keel-haul him.'

How appropriate that a man like Ivar had found this as his final resting place.

As the summer dusk slowly fell, the trees ranked densely to either side of them seemed to close in, to squeeze the green shadows in their dim, dusty depths. Somewhere close by, an osprey made its shrill, piping call. It was a cold, menacing sound, and it lingered long in the otherwise silent forest.

ᚠᛘᛝᚱ

The barrow was a ten-minute walk up through the woods, located on a truncated spur overlooking the crashing waves on the island's northern coast. It was perilously close to the cliff-edge, and exposed to the elements on all sides. As with many tumuli, it was little more than a rounded, grassy hummock, about 10 or 12 yards in length, but two things gave it away at once: the low tunnel dug several feet into its western end, and only partially sheltered by a small canvas awning, much of which flapped in tatters from its flexible aluminium frame, courtesy of the Cork University team's unsuccessful expedition in the January of that year; and the sentinel form of the megalith, a vertical granite obelisk standing 10 paces to the west. This was about nine feet tall, and covered in mosses and lichen, though it had clearly been squared off at the top, indicating that, by origin, it had been hacked from its own bedrock, probably for the very purpose of being put here. Additional evidence of this was the vague inscription on its surface. Further examination revealed Icelandic-style runes, though even after tearing away much of the vegetation and getting in close with her eye-glass, Professor Mercy was not immediately able to decipher anything.

'I think there's a reference here to Halfdan,' she said, pointing out one particular passage. 'He was one of Ivar's brothers, of course. But I can't be sure what else it says.'

Alan and Craig glanced at each other curiously; to come across a piece of Viking writing that Professor Mercy was unable to translate, was a new experience indeed.

A moment later, they were surveying the barrow itself.

'I wonder how deep the Cork lot actually got,' said Linda, raising her voice to be heard over the wind.

Craig crouched down. 'Let's check it out.'

A moment later, he had ventured forward under the awnings, and had thrust his head and shoulders into the dark mouth of the passageway. A second passed, there was some grunting, then he began to wriggle his gangling body forwards, until only his legs were visible.

'It's not bad,' came his muffled voice. He squirmed his way back out, and stood beating soil from his clothes. 'They got a fair way – about three or four feet, which, if it *is* hollow, must be fairly close to the central cavity. There's a heavy stone up, blocking any further access. Probably a portal.'

Professor Mercy considered this, then nodded. 'Good, very good,' she said, unslinging her pack.

Barry sneered. 'Imagine doing all that work then sodding off, just because of the weather.'

Clive shook his head. 'It can get pretty wild round here.' He licked a finger and held it up in the stiff wind. 'This is nothing, believe me.'

'Let's not waste the valuable sunshine, then,' the

Professor said, kneeling on the grass and laying out her tools. Though it was now late evening, she was clearly eager to get started.

They debated briefly, finally deciding that while there was still a couple of hours of daylight left, it wouldn't do any harm at least to try to enlarge the space around the portal-stone. As the previous party had already set timber struts up inside the tunnel, most of which appeared to be solid, this seemed a reasonable proposition. Among the Professor's various tools, she had a small hand-axe and a pick. Only one person could get into the access passage at a time, so Craig took these, along with a torch, and went in first. While he was doing this, the others busied themselves finding a flat area on which they could erect the field-lab. This would basically be an open-sided tent under which they could store their equipment, paperwork and any decent finds, though for the moment they'd left most of that gear down at the base-camp.

Half an hour later Craig re-emerged, filthy but full of enthusiasm. 'It's coming,' he said, wiping sweaty soil from his brow. 'It's a granite block, about as big as a portable TV. Another 10 minutes, though, and it's loose I reckon. We might be able to move it tonight.'

Nug took over, and sure enough, within just over 10 minutes, his muted but trembling voice called out that the stone was shifting ... at which point, the going got slightly tougher. As only one person could fit into the tunnel, this meant Nug had to haul the stone at least four feet on his own. As if the thing wasn't heavy enough, he'd have to do this crawling backwards on his hands and knees, which would be virtually impossible. The goal was achieved only when Barry and Alan took him by the feet and pulled him bodily out, Nug yelping and yowling, but dragging the stone along with him.

Even then it was a painfully slow process, but eventually worth the wait. For the stone, in itself, proved to be an exciting find. It was caked in impacted clay, which the professor gently crumbled off with her fingers while the others held it up; it took three of them to do this. The rest watched in tense, breathless silence, as the stone was finally laid down, and their project-leader kneeled to examine it more closely. It was clear that some kind of etching had been made on the stone's surface. As they did not yet have water and sponges at their disposal, Clive took what he liked to call his 'awl' – a long steel pin with a leather-bound handle – and delicately scraped away the detritus crusted into the grooves. It was five minutes or so before the image was fully visible; when it was, it appeared to be a snake-like creature, arranged in a pattern of typically symmetrical Nordic whorls. It had been chiselled with delicate skill and meticulous attention to detail.

'What is it, a sea-serpent or something?' David asked.

'I wouldn't think so,' Clive said. 'Can't imagine this is just decorative. To be cut on a portal-stone, it'll probably have some arcane significance.' He glanced up at the Professor. 'Any thoughts? Skadi's Viper, perhaps?'

She gave him a deep and meaningful look, and for a moment there was a faint tension between the two, a curious uncertainty about what they had, a wariness even. 'I suppose it shows we're on the right path,' she finally said. All of a sudden, she didn't seem quite so exhilarated.

Clive nodded and resumed his examination. In his case, too, guardedness had overcome enthusiasm. Alan watched them, perplexed. This find in itself would grace any national collection, never mind the items it might presage if it really *was* a portal-stone. He was about to ask them what was wrong when Nug re-emerged from the tunnel, irritable and coughing. 'Can't get through in there yet,' he complained loudly. 'There's more bloody soil in the way. Maybe a foot of it.'

Professor Mercy considered, then looked up at the darkling sky. 'Well ... it'll wait until tomorrow,' she said. 'I think we've done enough for one evening. Well done everyone. Let's pack up.'

They made their way back to the camp in their twos and threes, talking excitedly. Though still subdued, both Clive and the Professor seemed certain they were on the verge of something big. Nug was talking about knocking the spots off Sutton Hoo, Craig about having their very own exhibit in the British Museum. Alan walked alone, however, and in silence. He was just as keyed up as the rest, but now found himself racking his brains for any reference to Skadi's Viper. He'd asked about this briefly, before they'd knocked off, but neither Clive nor the Professor had chosen to elaborate, saying simply that it had been just a passing thought and was 'nothing important'. The student's knowledge of Norse mythology didn't extend half as far as either of theirs, but, oddly, he felt certain they weren't being entirely honest in this.

Skadi's Viper? ... He'd definitely heard that phrase somewhere before. And, as Clive had hinted, in some significant arcane respect.

ᚢᚱ

On every side of him the grey seas rose like Himalayan mountainsides, booming and awesome. He tilted sideways and thought he might go overboard, but somehow his feet remained planted firmly. An oak-like strength ran through him: he knew no fear; scarcely felt the cold, though the skies above were brittle with winter's breath, though the rigging-ropes thrumming in the strong salt wind were slick and hard with frost, though the great raven sail Land-Waster bellied and banged overhead.

Onward, the ornate prow rose and fell as it crested the swells. Through the breaking surf, a long green shore emerged, bleak and misted with the dawn. Beyond it stood the blue humps of mountains, their snowy heads lost in clots of cloud – though, as Alsvidh rose on his pillar of flame and glared through the cracks of the ice, torrents of hot crimson light spilled down the flowing screes, and the Jotuns beat their hammers on the walls of their deep Earth prison, and now Alan felt that immense surging in his veins.

Oh, how he wanted to tear it: to tear that land, to tear it up by its rock-roots, to bend and twist and turn it, to burst out its blood and entrails, its priests and nuns, its saints and relics, its simpering, cowardly kings, who hid behind their sacred swords and gilded thrones, their hearth-men and their adder pits. To tear and tear, to rip and smash and pummel until the thick silver fleece on the backs of his hands was drenched and matted with gore, 'til the black blades of his clenching claws glittered like dragon-fire ...

Alan awoke with a start.

For a moment he was befuddled and dazed, blinking hard in the deep blue light inside his tent. Then he turned over and yawned. As usual, the Fibrefill sleeping bag had kept him comfortably warm, while the foam mat, though always difficult at first, had gradually absorbed his weight and protected him from any dampness or ground-chill. Alan glanced at his watch. It read five o'clock, which was very early by his normal standards, but even though he'd not managed to get to sleep until around one that morning, he opted to rise. It was impossible not to, with the energy of the expedition, and the excitement of the find still pulsing through him.

Outside, the camp lay in blissful summer morning slumber. Below the line of the trees, the early sun gleamed on the bog-pools, while above, it broke through the dense pine canopy in misty, milky shafts. To Alan's surprise, Craig and David were already up and about. Craig, clad for climbing in his sweater, his cleated boots, his longest, thickest socks, a pair of woollen trousers and a red and white Llanelli bob-cap, was kneeling outside his own tent, enthusiastically stuffing goods into his day-sack; among other things, some rolled-up waterproofs, his camera, and a block of Kendal Mint Cake. He was proverbially bright-eyed and bushy-tailed. David, on the other hand, was pale with early-morning nausea, and, again showing his inexperience, standing around clad only in denims and sneakers, neither of which were suitable for this austere landscape.

'Don't tell me you're still going after that sea-eagle?' said Alan, strolling over. 'Not after yesterday?'

Craig nodded and grinned. 'You got it, bud. The Prof wants us up and at it by nine. Didn't see she could complain about me getting a little R and R *before* breakfast.'

Alan was genuinely amazed. 'We're on the brink of the archaeological find of the century, and you're going bird-watching?'

'It wouldn't be so bad if they were birds without feathers, would it,' David put in, with a wan smile.

Craig just laughed. 'You guys have your passions, I have mine.'

Alan glanced over the glen towards the high crags where the bird nested. 'Passion isn't the word for it. You sure you'll be able to get there and back in time?'

With a flourish, Craig zipped his sack up. 'Dunno. Got to suss it out first. Can't do that from down here, of course.' He glanced sideways at David. 'You still tagging along?'

David nodded. 'Mmm.' He looked at Alan and yawned. Up close, he was bug-eyed from lack of sleep. He rubbed wearily at what was probably a stiff neck.

'Never had you down for an ornithologist, Dave,' Alan said.

He shrugged. 'I'm not, but what else is there to do? I've been awake all night, picking bloody pine-cones out of my spine. Anything's better than doing that for another three hours.'

Craig stood and brushed a few needles from his knees. He then gave David's 'street-corner' clothing a dubious once-over. 'I hate to say this, but you'll not get far up in that gear.'

'I'm not going *up*, don't worry.' David's tone implied that the idea alone was ludicrous. 'Once we get off the flat, I'm leaving you to it. Support from below is *my* remit.'

Craig looked at Alan and shook his head. 'Support from below ... I ask you.'

Alan chuckled.

'Come on then, Sherpa Tensing,' Craig said, setting jauntily off, sack on back.

David grinned sleepily at Alan. 'It's great here, isn't it.' He wandered off in pursuit of Craig. 'I'm having about as much fun as a one-legged man in an arse-kicking contest ...'

Alan continued chuckling as he set about clearing the cold debris of the last fire, then gathering a few dry sticks and sprigs of fir to get the next one going. After that, he went for a walk. Perhaps inevitably, he found himself heading back towards the dig.

As he strolled, he thought only briefly about the odd dream he'd had. Vivid as it had been, its details were already fading in his memory. He could still feel something of the emotions it had inspired within him, however: a raw love of the wild; a fearlessness of Nature and a oneness with the savagery of its moods. He glanced up and breathed deeply of the fresh, heather-scented air. Craeghatir might have its own micro-climate within its secretive interior, but the sky above it possessed that vast, pale emptiness of the north Atlantic. There was a harsh brightness to the light here, a relentless ferocity about the seas heaving around the coasts, about the sub-Arctic winds howling over the high, gorse-laden crags.

When he got back up beside the barrow, it was everything he'd expected it to be. The view from the cliff-side was incredible: the awesome, rolling wastes of the northern ocean, the way the surf rose up in fountains from the occasional rocks and skerries. The sun was high and hot, yet up here it barely registered in the strong northerly breeze. Despite the Vikings' atrocities, it was difficult to hate anyone who had spread the hand of conquest over so wild and uncharted a portion of the world as this. All kinds of wonderful stories abounded about how the Northmen had mastered this most hostile of environments, breaking out from the ice-bound fjords of their homeland by following the paths of whales or hacking compasses from the magnetic cores of fallen meteorites; or by navigating rivers into the deepest wildernesses of Europe and Asia's continental interiors, and, inspired by their ferocious gods, battling and defeating anyone who came against them, no matter how superior the numbers. At the time there'd seemed no limit to their achievements, either spiritually or geographically. Legends told how they'd even reached Africa and the Americas. Good Lord ... four of the world's seven continents contacted five centuries before Columbus, and with what? Crude weapons and flimsy longships.

Yes ... it was difficult, if not impossible, to hate any race of men who could achieve so much with so little. To fear them, on the other hand? That was a different matter. Fearing them was easily possible. And in that moment, like a dash of cold water, Alan remembered exactly where he'd heard about Skadi's Viper.

And it had everything to do with fear.

Wonderingly, he walked away from the precipice to the tunnel mouth, where the portal-stone still lay on its tarpaulin bed. In the bright morning light, the carved serpent looked even more beautiful than it had before, the endless coils of its body interwoven with near mathematical precision, filling almost every inch of the exposed surface.

Skadi's Viper … indeed; in fact, now that he thought about it, without any doubt at all.

The story concerned Loki, the Norse god of Evil. It told how, weary of his many crimes and fearful of what he might do next, the other gods took Loki and bound him in perdition with mighty chains; the goddess Skadi then added to these a poisonous serpent or viper, a creature so monstrous that it was thought no-one and nothing could escape its clutches. According to the legend, of course, that thinking proved incorrect.

Alan regarded the stone with a new fascination, and then he thought about the opened barrow behind him, and how this too had been incarceration of a sort. He chuckled, genuinely amused.

All the same, there was a faint but undeniable chill in the pit of his stomach.

ᚼᛁᛦ

Linda was knee-deep in the water, bathing.
Alan came up to the shoreline and watched her for a moment. He wasn't sure if she was aware of him. As the rest of the camp was still fast asleep, she had stripped down to a pair of skimpy knickers and, though the water was evidently cold, she was luxuriating in its cleansing caresses. She had produced a sponge from somewhere, and was working it slowly over every shining inch of her supple, athletic form. As he watched, her thin cotton panties turned filmy and transparent. The arousal this brought him was agonising in its intensity.

'So you're a voyeur now?' she suddenly asked, without turning to look at him.

'Is that a problem?' he wondered, nervously.

Linda smiled to herself. 'I doubt it would look good on a CV.'

Her apparent lack of concern gave him new courage. 'I mean is it a problem for *you* ... me watching?'

In response, she rolled the sponge over her small, firm breasts, the peaks of which came perkily erect. 'It's nothing you haven't seen before, I suppose.'

'That isn't answering the question,' Alan said,

drawing his t-shirt over his head.

She made no reply; didn't even seem to notice as he unlaced his boots, kicked them off, removed his socks, then waded out into the pool in his corduroy pants. Now she turned to face him, apparently surprised, though whether this was in pretence or not, he couldn't tell. She folded her arms across her breasts, though dark fur was clearly visible through her soaked underwear.

'What do you want?' she said, as he came up to her.

Alan gazed boldly down at her. 'What do you think?'

Suddenly she looked innocent, child-like. Despite the warm sunlight, she was shivering. 'I thought we agreed ...'

'We agreed nothing,' he interjected. 'I told you, that incident at the party was a complete mistake ... I owned up to it straight away, didn't I?'

Linda stared up at him for a few seconds, uncertain. Then she made a move away. 'I think it's better if we just forget everything ...'

Alan took her by the elbow, gently but firmly. 'I don't think that's possible, Linda.'

She turned to face him again, and glanced nervously over his shoulder towards the silent camp. 'Alan ... I'm seeing someone else, now.'

'And I bet you're really enjoying it,' he replied.

She stared up at him again, and for a fleeting moment all the scorn and sarcasm and phony toughness was gone. Instead, she looked hurt beyond belief; in that brief second, he saw the welter of harm and misery he'd heaped upon her, not just through that foolish instant of lustful indiscretion and the horrific moment of truth when he'd finally, guiltily owned up to it, but through the aftermath of it as well; the forlorn desert of betrayal where he'd suddenly dumped her, alone, humiliated, heartlessly abandoned to the first boor who might happen along.

What was past was past, people said; you couldn't roll back time. Sins could be forgiven no matter what their severity, but could wounds really be healed ... deep wounds, which left you emotionally shattered? And at what point did reconciliation become exploitation? Alan knew only one thing, though ... after three weeks, it had been too long already. Way too long.

Slowly, he ran his hand down her cold, flat belly 'til he reached the band of her panties. It didn't stop him. He pushed his hand under and pressed on down. Still she gazed up at him, bewildered, injured. A moment later, he was running a single finger through her silky folds, already moist and warm. She finally reacted at that and tried to hit him. He caught her arm, however, and kissed her, crushing her body to his.

Only a split-second passed before she responded fiercely, throwing her arms around his shoulders, reaching up on tip-toes in the lapping, sun-dashed water ...

It was shortly after breakfast, when the group decided not to wait for those still out and about. The lure of the barrow was too strong. Whatever everyone was up to, the Professor said, it would be *their* loss.

The final blockage of soil proved stubborn indeed. Presumably packed into place as a form of primitive cement for the portal-stone, it had been strengthened with pebbles and braced by wicker-work cross-pieces. The Professor, Nug, Clive and Barry each took turns to hack and cut at it with the pick and hand-axe, which in the cramped confines of the unlit tunnel became an ordeal in itself. As the outside temperature rose, so it rose inside the hole, until it was stifling and airless. What was worse, much of the impacted earth was so dry that, once disturbed, it tended to fill the air in a black, gritty fog. As someone remarked, between coughs and wheezes, 'you'd be better wearing a gas-mask down there'.

The entire thing entailed almost an hour of such strenuous, unrelenting work. But they kept at it, tirelessly, encouraged all the way by the sure knowledge that their goal was just within reach.

Alan and Linda lay together on a lush and springy mattress of marsh marigolds.

They kissed deeply, hungrily, their tongues entwined, sinuous as serpents. Blissful, seemingly endless moments followed, broken only when it suddenly struck the girl that her briefs had now come off entirely and that she was completely naked in the arms of her former lover.

'This ... this is wrong,' she moaned, trying half-heartedly to pull away from him.

Alan refused to release her. 'This is exactly the opposite of wrong. This is the way it should be, and you know it.'

'We can't ...'

He ran his lips across her throat. 'You want it and I want it. Who says we can't?'

It was too much for her. After several weeks of abstention, and the subsequent yearning desire, which the loyal, puppy-like presence of Barry had done nothing to dispel, the heated presence of the male she had shared her bed so rapturously with for so long, was overwhelming. She dropped back and allowed his hot mouth free range across her body, the darting tongue licking at and teasing her stiffly swollen nipples, swirling around then burrowing into her tight navel, drawing wet trails along the insides of her thighs, and finally plunging into her, probing between petals of warm, tangy flesh and finally mounting her clitoral hood, where it spun in wicked little spirals.

Deep shudders passed through the girl as her nectar flooded across the boy's mouth, as she clawed and raked at him, leaving fiery striations with her fingernails. A moment later, she struggled free and rent at the front of his trousers, yanking them down past his knees, wrenching the underpants after them, engulfing him in a single, voracious swallow. Alan felt his cockhead nudge the very back of her throat. He gasped aloud and rose up on his knees, hands clenching her shoulders. The girl rode back and forth, stropping him with her lips, sucking him with such intensity that he thought he was going to faint.

When he seeped hot pre-cum into her mouth, she groaned in pleasure and teased his glans with her teeth.

When the plug finally broke, the first thing they knew was a sour odour from within ... perhaps inevitably; it was the stale vapour of a sealed-in millennium. It lasted no longer than a minute, however, and a tiny fissure – no more than a handful of soil knocked through into empty blackness by two thrusting fingers – was sufficient to let it escape.

After that, the job became easy. Again, they took it in

turns, now working with a new energy, each one of them sweating buckets in the tight passage, but plunging and plunging at the diminishing obstruction with their hands and tools, widening and deepening the crevice, until it was almost a perfect continuation of the entrance-tunnel, an archway that even the largest and most ungainly member of the party could pass through with relative ease.

   Of course, they'd been working in complete darkness, so even when the doorway was finished, it was uncertain what might await them in the unlit gulf beyond it.

Linda locked her ankles behind Alan's back, which gave her greater leverage to lift herself bodily up and meet his urgent thrusts. For his own part, Alan's erection felt hard and thick as steel. He worked it in and out of her with a slippery, smooth motion, reaching new depths of penetration with each and every push, probing the very core of her being it seemed, for as Linda orgasmed, powerfully, she gasped and squealed aloud. It was a fortunate thing they'd managed to carry each other 100 yards at least along the shore of the bog-pools, before they'd finally lost control and gone at each other like beggars at the banquet, for neither had been able to suppress the sounds of passion for long.

   Still, Alan slid back and forth in her vaginal grip, his prick seeming to lengthen and strengthen with every stroke. Wordlessly, Linda complied, at each turn finding greater, hotter depths in which to accommodate him. Like the rest of her body, she was taut and strong down there; at one moment, her pussy was soft and pliable so that it flowed around his rigid member like warm, melted butter, at the next, its muscles tightened to an alarming degree, seizing his shaft in a crushing fist, determined to milk it for every drop of fluid it possessed. Again, it was too much. Heady, swooning with the joy of it, he arched his back and let go.

A second stream followed and a third. Alan arched his back again and gave a strangled cry, Linda a low, heart-felt moan as her womb was flooded ...

'*Oooh man!*' came an ecstatic voice.

They all waited expectantly as Nug crawled out from the entrance, beating the dirt from his arms and t-shirt. He was slick with sweat and his pallor had increased, but his bearded face was a picture of barely suppressed delight. 'You've *got* to go in there, folks ... just check it out!'

The professor took the torch and a camera and went in next, Clive following close behind. The others would have to wait their turn as Nug reckoned that only two people could fit inside the burial chamber at any one time and preserve the integrity of the find. But they all got their chance.

Once they'd crawled along the access tunnel, and squeezed through the freshly dug circular hole at the end of it, they found themselves inside a rectangular, even-sided compartment formed by interlocking slabs of stone set up like a box. At roughly six feet by four, and with a ceiling only three feet from the ground, it was incredibly claustrophobic, while the stuffy, putrid atmosphere, though breathable, was still fairly revolting. All these discomforts, however, were more than made up for by what the compartment contained.

Their first thought was that it was the most

important archaeological discovery in modern times; their second, that they'd need a full research team here on Craeghatir and that a few weeks this summer would not be nearly enough to complete what was potentially the most sensational project of any of their careers.

At first glance, the whole place was thick with drapes of web, while a dense shroud of grey dust lay over a variety of objects on the floor. This shroud was perfectly smooth, like an undisturbed blanket, but it didn't conceal the objects' worth. For example, towards the far end of the chamber, the intruders' torchlight immediately picked out the corroded iron nose-piece and cheek-guards of a full-head Dark Age helmet. Then it glittered on the hoard of silver coins laid out all around it … on ingots and bangles, on brooches, pins and scattered gemstones, evidently all spilled from sacks which had long ago rotted to nothing.

Exhilarated, barely able to speak, the team recorded everything on film and then went hurriedly to work with their brushes. They'd hardly dared hope for more, but they found it nevertheless, and within a matter of minutes. Below the helmet there was a skull … it lay in desiccated fragments, but it was clearly identifiable as a skull. Further down the body, the relics of ribs and folded arm-bones were visible, still clad in tarnished ring-mail. On top of these, the iron boss was all that remained of a circular linden-wood shield, but there was also the skeleton of a once-fabulous broadsword, the blade now crooked and coated in rust, but still fitted into its decorative cross-hilt.

To a man and woman, the team were so shaken with the trove, each member so absorbed in what he or she was doing that at first they worked entirely in silence, the only sound the steady dripping of sweat as they cleaned and polished feverishly. But when they came out into the open air again, their glee gave way like an over-laden dam; they whooped and screamed, danced wild jigs with each other, threw themselves around in wild and manic abandon until Craeghatir's highest ridges and deepest, darkest groves of woodland fairly rang to the echoes.

Alan and Linda stared at each other breathless across the crushed straggle of marigolds. As the morning had worn on, insects had come to life around them. There was now a faint humming of bees, a shrill whine of midges. Linda ignored them all. Her gaze bored into Alan like a drill-bit into stone. There was guilt there, that was true ... but there was also a gleam of angry accusation.

'You're a son of a bitch,' she said quietly.

'For God's sake, Linda ...'

Alan leaned over and offered her his hand, but she chose to ignore it. In fact, she flinched away. 'Don't come near me again!'

'You were as keen as I was,' he protested.

'I'm not denying it.' Hurriedly, she started to dress. 'But it's over now, definitely.'

Alan watched helplessly as she climbed quickly into her trousers, then pulled her sweat-top down over her bare, still deeply-flushed breasts.

'Look,' he said, 'I didn't ... I mean, I *don't* just want you for sex.'

She gave him a hard, unsympathetic look as she grabbed up her socks and boots. 'It doesn't matter what *you* want, Alan. All that's over, I've told you. I've found a new life now, and you should too.'

'This is insane,' he said, rising to his knees, trying to stop her. She weaved her way past him, however, and set off barefoot back towards the camp. 'Linda ... wait!'

'The others'll be up by now, we've got to get back,' she said over her shoulder. 'And for Christ's sake, don't follow me straight away ... give me five minutes first.'

He watched her go mournfully. He'd like to have thought he'd be surprised by this, stunned even. But in truth he wasn't. Linda was an emotional girl, but she didn't hang by those emotions. Anyone who deliberately bruised her could expect serious and prolonged payback. Not necessarily indefinitely, of course. She wasn't that much of a basket-case – but while genuine contrition might eventually pave the way to forgiveness, raw animal lust certainly wouldn't, no matter how neglected the girl's own needs happened to be.

Alan gave Linda a good 10 minutes, before he ventured back himself. When he finally got there, he found the rest of the group in a state of intense excitement; so much so that no-one at all seemed to question their absence.

One after another, artifacts were brought out of the chamber which defied any but the most optimistic level of expectation. The Professor herself uncovered two axe-heads carved all over with symbols of the *Aesir*; Clive found a gilded bronze casket containing chess pieces fashioned from walrus ivory. Everywhere they searched inside the tomb there were priceless items. Barry – big clumsy Barry, came up with ornaments cut from jet, jade and bluestone. Immediately after that, Linda found a horse-collar of solid gold. There were emeralds as well, rubies, sapphires, superb objects worked in amber, antler, amethyst. As the Professor said, whoever it was that had been buried here, he'd sought to take his entire wealth to eternity with him. And as Nug replied, that definitely sounded like Ivar.

Alan, though as impressed as everyone else, was finding it hard to share in their joy. Throughout the dig, in the midst of shouts and shrieks of amazed laughter, he remained distracted by the events of earlier that morning, and several times tried to get close enough to Linda to speak privately to her. For her part, the girl seemed to have thrown herself back into the mission with a vengeance. It was just before lunchtime, and she was sitting cross-legged beside the field-lab, dusting down a small idol, when he finally came up and crouched next to her.

'Hi,' he said, keeping his voice low.

She glanced at him, then continued with her work. 'Seen this?' She held the idol up for his inspection. 'Gerde, the giantess. The Prof reckons it's solid silver. I'll tell you, we're re-writing archaeological history here.'

'Yeah. Very nice ...'

'She's talking about getting a forensic pathologist over, to date the bones. That'll strengthen the case for this being ...'

'Look, sod the bloody bones!'

Alan hadn't meant to raise his voice, but it simply came out that way. He looked worriedly around, but none of the others seemed to have heard. Linda, on the other hand, was regarding him coldly, her mouth clamped shut like a trap.

'I want to talk about this morning,' he said after a moment.

She made no reply.

'I'm ... well, I'm sorry.' He hung his head. 'For what it's worth. I thought ... you know, I thought you were fully consenting ... I thought the whole thing was above board.'

A moment passed, then Linda got on with her brushing. 'It was.'

'So ... what's the problem?'

'Like I say,' she replied, 'forget it.'

'How can I?'

'Try!'

'I can't.'

'Well try harder!' she snapped, finally rounding on him. 'I have and it's worked a treat. Because, do you know what? Nothing happened this morning, Alan. Nothing at all. I got up, you got up. The day commenced.'

She made a show of getting to her feet, but he did the same and grabbed her by the wrist. 'So now we're in fucking denial, are we!'

She yanked herself free, at last furious with him. 'Don't you dare talk to me like that! Ever!'

And she stormed away over the top of the ridge, stopping only to plonk the idol down in the specimens tray. Alan followed her, no longer worried about drawing attention to himself.

'Linda ... come on,' he pleaded. 'I've said I'm sorry. Just come back, eh. Come on.'

'I'm busy,' she said through gritted teeth.

'I'll do anything ...'

'Then leave me alone,' she hissed. And with that she was gone, hurrying away down the hillside towards the outer cover of the pines, finally breaking into a run.

Alan was left there like a spare part, staring after her,

as bewildered as he was crestfallen. And then, suddenly, unexpectedly, there was a voice in his ear, murmuring quietly. 'Look ... Alan, I don't want to make a big thing out of this ...' Alan turned sharply, to find Clive there, a disapproving frown on his broad, normally genial features. 'But, listen, we're going to be pretty busy over the next few days. So the last thing we need is stresses and strains in the ranks ...'

'Yeah, well it's fucking all right for you, isn't it!' Alan retorted aggressively. 'I mean you're fixed up aren't you, Clive. You've got Miss Bloody ... Bloody ...'

And then it came back to him: *reality*, swimming around him as though a fog had suddenly lifted. This wasn't just a tutor he was talking so rudely to, but a friend and colleague, someone who'd been with him, providing care and guidance, since pre-grad. On top of that, it was also someone who'd be marking his end-of-course papers, who'd be assessing his general performance, both in the class and in the field, someone who'd be making recommendations and references. In short, someone who was in a very good position to damage Alan's prospects for further advancement, if he so desired. Not that this was Clive's style, but beneath the cuddly, loveable exterior, they'd always suspected there'd be a bullish core, and now, briefly, it showed itself. The tutor's expression hardened; his normally grinning mouth curled the other way for once. His private life was strictly off-limits. That was one area in which he notoriously took no prisoners, especially in relation to his out-of-hours contacts with Professor Mercy. He and she were the worst-kept secret on campus, but woe betide anyone who started blabbing about it.

Hurriedly, Alan held up his hands. 'Okay ... okay.

Sorry. Well out of order, and I know it. Just a bit stressed ... All this excitement, you know.'

Clive said nothing. Simply stared him out for a few seconds, then gave a curt nod and ambled away. When he'd gone, Alan glanced around worriedly, wondering who else's cage he might have rattled. There was no sign of Barry; he was probably inside the barrow ... which was something of a relief, no matter how unimportant Alan held him to be. Nug was leaning over a table up at the field-lab, studiously involved in something; his back was firmly turned. And of course, Craig and David hadn't showed up yet from their morning's excursion. That left only Professor Mercy. She was over by the megalith, studying the inscription there. She too seemed to be preoccupied, but Alan knew it wasn't his imagination that she was scrutinising him from the corner of her eye.

'Fuck,' he said under his breath. 'Fuck, fuck fuck ...'

ᚺᛗᛝᛗᚠ

It was shortly after one o'clock when David reappeared, still yawning, scratching his overhanging belly as he sauntered lazily through the trees.

'Wow,' he said. 'Something smells good.'

Nug nodded. 'It was.'

'Uh?' David glanced around, non-plussed. There was no sign of the fried bacon he'd been sniffing. In fact, the fire had been doused. Everyone else now seemed to be wrapping up their plates, and laying out their tools again.

'Lunch is finished, David,' Professor Mercy said.

'Oh, come on ...' he protested.

'Where've you been all day?'

'Oh.' He rubbed his brow. A yellow crust of sleep was still visible under each of his eyes. 'Er ... sorry about that. Didn't get much kip last night. Ended up dozing off on a nice patch of dry grass. Totally lost track of time.'

She pursed her lips as she considered.

David looked round hungrily. 'I accept I've missed the fry-up, but is there *anything* going? I'm starving.'

Clive tossed him a packet of peanuts. 'Here. These'll help keep your energy up.'

David examined the snack disconsolately, as the rest of them got their equipment together. 'It's a laugh a minute, this, isn't it,' he finally said.

'How can you think of food on a dig as exciting as this?' wondered Nug.

'Listen pal, I can think of food at any time,' was David's tart reply.

'Where's Craig anyway?' the Professor asked him.

He looked up at her, surprised. 'Isn't he here?'

There was a brief silence, then Alan came forward. 'What do you mean, 'Isn't he here'? He was with you.'

'Only for about 20 minutes,' David replied. 'The moment he started climbing, I sloped off. Been wandering around the island, sight-seeing. Like I say, I finally ended up nodding off.'

Professor Mercy gazed at him for a moment, then turned to Alan. 'Craig went climbing alone?'

Alan made a helpless gesture. 'Well yeah … but it's not as if he's inexperienced, is it?'

By this time, everybody else was listening. There'd been no sign of Craig Barker since most of them had woken up.

'I don't care how experienced he is,' the Professor said. 'Solo climbs are risky. You *know* that, Alan.'

'I doubt he'll try and tackle any rock-faces,' David offered. 'I mean, he hasn't got the ropes or pins or anything.'

Alan shook his head. 'Craig climbs freestyle.'

'What time did he set off?' the Professor asked.

'Five-ish,' Alan replied. 'Said he'd be back for breakfast.'

She turned to David again. 'And *you* definitely haven't seen him?'

David shook his head.

'He's probably just lost track of time,' Alan put in. 'I'll find him.'

The Professor nodded. 'David, go with him, please. Show him exactly where Craig went. And get a move on, can you, lads. We've had only half a team on all morning, as it is.'

The two of them made their way speedily downhill, slogged around the western edge of the bog-pools, passed the cave and were soon walking back uphill via the island's inner southern slope.

'I just assumed he'd be all right,' said David, after a few moments.

'He probably is, don't worry,' Alan replied.

'I mean, there wouldn't have been much I could have helped him with, anyway.'

'I know. Like I say ... don't worry.'

They proceeded in silence, tense minutes passing as they pressed on, threading between the trees, breathing progressively harder. Sweat started to bead their brows as the slope angled steeply upwards.

'I'm pretty sure we went *this* way,' said David, veering towards the left but still ascending.

Forty yards ahead, the ground rose up into an almost sheer gradient of roots and broken earth. They'd come perhaps 1,000 yards from the camp, and the pine cover had thinned out dramatically, until only one or two of the sturdiest specimens remained. Not far beyond those, the slope suddenly transformed into a vertical wall of rock, which climbed tier upon tier towards the azure sky.

'I'd left him to it by this time,' said David, leaning forwards, panting. 'I assume he went straight on.'

Alan shielded his eyes to gaze upwards, hoping against hope that he'd spy Craig's lanky frame coming gracefully down, leaping from ledge to ledge in that carefree, goat-like manner that he had, a big cherubic grin on his wholesome Welsh face. There was no such sign. The thought was reassuring, however, that their pal – who, of course, on this first ascent had not intended to get all the way up to the eagle's nest – had let his enthusiasm get the better of him, and had kept on going, finally finding a fantastic angle on the eyrie, and was now snapping shot after shot. That would certainly be like the ornithologist, though he was generally more responsible than to while away so many hours without at least letting someone know where he was.

Alan scrambled forwards again, not exactly sure where he was going to go from this point; unlike Craig, he had minimal skills on the rock-face, but he was urgently aware that he had to get a result of some kind. It was now well into the afternoon, and the sun was at its zenith.

It was this that gave them their first clue.

It threw a misshapen shadow onto the cliff-face. At first it was an amorphous blot, a confluence of branches twisted here, there and everywhere, tangling themselves in a knot at the centre. The more Alan stared up at this, however, the more he fancied he could see human limbs inside it – limp and dangling, maybe the indistinct outline of a lolling human head. Suddenly, a bolt of terror went through him. Alan stopped dead and turned, gazing up into the trees behind them. David did the same.

Horror jolted the pair of them, violently.

Craig was up there, hanging from one of the higher boughs – not by his hands, or by a piece of clothing caught on a twig, or even by a rope. He was hanging from the branch because he'd been bent over it. Backwards. It was a horrible and yet impossible sight. The back of Craig's head almost touched the backs of his heels. It was as if he had no spine at all. He'd simply been thrown over the branch and draped there like a wet towel. Even from far below, they could see that his rigid face bore an expression of excruciating pain. His camera still hung by its strap from one of his dangling wrists.

'Oh my God ...' David breathed, scarcely audible.

A second of stunned silence passed, then Alan jerked into action. 'Quickly!' he said. 'Give me a hand.' He dashed forward, jumped for one of the lower branches and tried to haul himself up.

'But he must be dead,' David protested.

'We don't know that.'

'Know it? But he's been folded up like a piece of paper ...'

'David!' Alan shouted. 'Just get your arse over here and give me a hand!'

David hurried to comply, and at last Alan got a decent purchase, swung himself up and began to climb properly. He went up steadily, moving from one gnarled limb to the next. Ten feet, 20 feet ... He continued to clamber, never once looking down, oblivious to the soon-precipitous drop below him; not because he was naturally fearless, or even because he was particularly good at climbing trees, but because the circumstances wouldn't allow it. He knew only one thing – that he had to get up alongside Craig in order to discover that the casualty was actually okay, that it looked far worse than it was, maybe even that the Welsh guy was shamming, just playing a sick joke on them.

But long before he reached the jack-knifed form, he knew this wouldn't be the case.

Craig hung in a posture for which humanity had never been intended. As David had said, he'd literally been folded in two. The only explanation was that his backbone had snapped, probably with the impact on the heavy branch.

Alan finally got alongside his friend, and shinned out towards him. Hurriedly, he reached down and took Craig's wrist in his fingers. There was no pulse he could detect; the flesh was stone-cold. Alan let the hand drop and peered upwards. There was maybe 20 yards of open air between this tree and the rock-face, and as the rock-face ascended it leaned further and further away. It was difficult to see how Craig could have hit the tree at all in a straightforward fall. But then, one never knew. On such a slope, at such an angle, spaces could be deceptive. One thing was certain: Craig was not shamming.

'Shall I go and get the others?' David called up.

'You ... you might as well,' Alan replied, trying to keep his voice steady.

David hurried off down the slope, leaving him there alone ... which was something of a relief. Alan was at last able to hang his head. Tears squeezed out onto his cheeks. It was hardly the manly response to a crisis, but after all the emotional turbulence of the morning, this was the last thing he needed. On top of that, of course, there was shock. He'd never known anyone of his own age who'd died before; only now was the numbing realisation seeping through him that Craig Barker, a buddy since his first week in college, would never again figure in his life; that a few hours ago the cheeky chappie from South Wales had been healthy and perky as a spring-lamb, and that now it was all over and he was gone. They hadn't even had the chance to say 'See you'.

Several minutes passed as Alan silently wept, at the end of which time he struggled to get it back together. He couldn't afford to let the others see him like this. In addition, there were things he had to do. Like, somehow, get Craig's body down to ground level.

It wasn't going to be easy, but the problem was solved for him; as he took hold of Craig's trouser belt and tried to lug him along the branch towards the main trunk, the body dislodged and slid free. It fell heavily but limply, twisting and turning as it plummeted the remaining 30 or so feet to the ground. Alan winced at the sound of the collision, even though he knew that Craig was far past the point of pain.

It took him another five minutes to get himself down safely, and even then there were one or two hair-raising moments, smaller boughs bending or cracking beneath his boots, his hands occasionally losing their grip on the flaking, silver-gray bark. At long last, however, he touched down, then walked over to where Craig lay. The Welshman had landed on his back again, his arms and legs splayed out, his neck to one side. One of his eyelids had opened slightly, the already-yellowing orb visible below it. The mouth was still twisted in a rictal grimace of pain. There was a horrible rigidity about that final ugly expression – it was like an image carved from wax, rather than a human face.

Alan gazed helplessly at it for several more minutes. He was still doing so when the others arrived, scrambling up through the trees, David at their forefront. The students gathered around in stunned silence, while Professor Mercy and Clive attended to the body, checking the carotid artery at the side of the exposed throat, planting ears against the narrow, motionless chest. No check they made came up positive, however.

Another minute seemed to pass before anyone spoke. The tutors were standing up again as Alan began a long rambling explanation about how and where they'd found Craig, and how he'd accidentally knocked the body to the ground while trying to recover it. His words petered out as Clive hunkered down and checked again for vital signs, still to no avail.

Eventually, Professor Mercy looked up and gazed around at them. Her expression was difficult to read. Linda, on the other hand, was visibly upset, her green eyes glazed with tears. Nug was grim, David still white-faced. For all his usual bravado, even Barry Wood seemed shaken up.

'This is a bitter lesson to us all,' the Professor finally said. 'It just shows … this is not some holiday idyll. This is wild countryside and we're out on our own in it. From now on, recreational activities are out, okay? No exceptions.'

Alan looked up at her in surprise. 'From now on? You mean we're going on with the dig?'

She shrugged. 'What else can we do?'

'But surely we're at least going to call someone?' he said. 'I mean, the Coast Guard for instance. McEndry said we could …'

The Professor eyed him keenly. 'Why should we alert the Coast Guard? Nobody's in danger, nobody needs rescuing.'

Alan was astounded. 'But someone's just died!'

'People die all the time, Alan,' she replied. 'Accidents happen. It's terrible, I admit, tragic, but we've got a boat coming on Thursday evening. We don't need to call the Coast Guard.'

'Don't you think we should at least report it?'

'We will do,' she said. 'As soon as one of us gets back to the mainland.'

'I don't believe I'm hearing this ...'

Now Barry Wood stepped in. Inevitably, because the Professor was occupying a position contrary to Alan's, he was on her side. 'There's nothing anyone can do, is there?' he said. 'No-one can bring him back.'

Alan looked from one to the other. 'So you're saying we just carry on as though nothing's happened?'

'We'll put Craig in the monks' cave for the moment,' the Professor replied. 'No sense in burying him when we'll be out of here soon ...'

'Are you serious?' Alan turned for support from some of the others. 'Surely I'm not the only one here who thinks we should call for help?'

Clive looked uncertain. 'It's legally beholden on us to report the incident, of course,' he said.

'But that would mean making the find public knowledge before we've even half excavated it,' the Professor replied. Now Alan caught a glimmer of the way she was rationalising the tragedy. It both horrified and sickened him.

Clive nodded to himself. 'That must be a consideration.'

'Why don't we take a vote?' said Barry.

Alan was incredulous. 'A vote?'

'On whether we carry on, or call for McEndry to come early.'

'*For Christ's sake, someone has just died!*'

'Yes, but this is the find of the century, we're sitting on here,' the Professor argued. 'The last thing we need now is the press crawling all over the island, not to mention souvenir hunters.'

Alan found himself staring at her in disbelief and no little disgust; a stare she returned intently. For a fleeting moment, it was like he was looking at someone else, someone who also had beauty and power, but who had ice running through her veins instead of blood, who had a thing of iron where her heart should be. It was a side of her that he – in fact any of them – had never seen before.

'I can understand your position, Jo,' Nug finally said, in the stress of the moment using the Professor's first name. 'But while we've got the means to contact the authorities, people are certainly going to wonder why we didn't.'

'Of course they are,' Alan added. 'Even a couple of days' delay, and they'll be asking questions.'

For the first time, the Professor seemed unsure of her position. She gazed thoughtfully down at the body, then glanced sidelong at Clive. 'They have a point, I suppose,' he finally said. 'People *will* ask questions, and if it turns out we've delayed because we were too busy with the find, it won't look good.'

Again, she relapsed into thought, though clearly Clive's reasoning had made sense to her. 'All right,' she eventually said. 'We'll inform the Coast Guard station. This isn't an emergency, so it'll probably take them a day or so to get out here, anyway. Come on. Help me get something to cover him with.'

And with that, she turned and set off back towards the camp. The others went with her, all except Alan and Nug, the latter of whom now sank onto his haunches.

'Jesus,' Alan said, half to himself, 'talk about priorities.'

Nug, however, wasn't listening. He was crouching by the corpse, staring at it, a far-away look on his face. Finally, he stood up and turned. 'Listen, I don't particularly think there's anything in this, but you're sure Craig's death was an accident?'

Alan raised an eyebrow. 'Well ... obviously. I mean, he must have fallen. It's hard to see how he could have hit the tree, but what else could have happened?'

Nug stared up at the rock-face. 'It's just that ... well, this is obviously a big coincidence, but his spine's been broken, yeah?'

'I think so.'

Nug mused on this. 'If he'd fallen down through the upper branches, wouldn't there be other marks on him, cuts, grazes and such?'

'I suppose.'

'And there aren't.'

'What are you saying, Nug?' Alan was suddenly too tired for word-games.

Nug looked him in the eye. 'Ivar Ragnarsson sacrificed Mael Guala, the king of Munster, to the gods, by having his back ritually broken over a millstone, then hanging his body from a tree.'

Mixht

They wrapped Craig's twisted body in the groundsheet of his tent, then zipped him into his sleeping bag, before carrying him down the slope and finally depositing him just inside the mouth of the cave.

There was no ceremony, no-one made a speech or said any words. It was a forlorn and desolate little moment as they laid him there, but it occurred to Alan how much Ivar the Boneless would have approved. The Christianity the ferocious Dane had striven so hard to destroy by sheer barbarism, had eventually fallen to sophistication; the Godless wilderness he'd sought to create with fire and sword, had finally arrived through discussion and intellectualism. Such, it seemed, was the prize of progress.

Alan stood there for a moment, looking down at the shrouded form. Then he glanced up into the opaque darkness at the back of the cave. 'Perhaps we should move him further in?' he said. 'We don't want some animal to come and mess with the body.'

'And what kind of animal would that be?' Barry Wood scoffed. 'A grizzly bear?'

Alan turned sharply to face him. 'Do you have to try and score points off everything!'

Barry sneered in response. 'Do you have to find problems with everything!'

'I think we've got problems enough, without having to find them!'

'Will you two pack it in!' the Professor snapped. 'This is an upsetting incident, but we can only put it behind us and get on with our work if we stick together as a team. Now just simmer down, the pair of you.'

The two students backed off and did as they were told, Barry moving over to Linda, putting an arm around her, Alan finding solace in Nug's company. One by one, the group drifted out of the cave, making their tired, uneasy way back around the bog-pools towards the encampment. Eventually, only Alan and Nug remained.

'He was a good lad,' Alan said. 'A bit obsessive at times, but a good lad. There was certainly no evil in him.'

'He didn't deserve a death like that, that's for sure,' Nug replied. Then he glanced up. 'So what do you think?'

'About what?'

'About what I told you.'

Alan gave him a quizzical stare. 'I never had you down for the superstitious type.'

Nug shrugged. 'I'm not. It's just, well, this whole business seems wrong to me.'

Alan was about to reply, when they heard raised, heated voices from the direction of the tents. They looked at each other, then dashed out of the cave and scurried around the marsh, trying not to muddy themselves any more than they already had, in the process.

Two minutes later, they were back in the camp. The

first person they met was David. He had a pale, vaguely child-like look about him. 'You're not going to believe this,' he blurted out. 'The satellite phone's gone.'

Alan felt his hair prickle. 'What?'

The others were standing around between the tents, gazing at each other in bewilderment. Professor Mercy stood in the centre, holding the waterproof satchel, which was now open and empty.

'I'll ask again,' she demanded of them, 'is someone playing some kind of joke?'

'It's a bloody unfunny one, if they are!' said Nug.

'Where was it?' Alan asked.

She threw the empty sack on the floor. 'In the satchel, along with my mobile.'

'Has that gone too?'

Clive nodded grimly. 'They both have.'

'There's a surprise,' said Alan.

The Professor glanced sharply up at him. 'And what's that supposed to mean?'

He shrugged and waved it away. 'Nothing ... I'm just getting paranoid. Look, Craig had a phone, didn't he?'

There were a few mumbles in the positive. Uncomfortable glances were then exchanged.

'Well *someone* had better go and get it,' Linda finally said.

No-one moved, until Alan lurched off back in the direction of the cave. Dejectedly, Nug went with him.

Getting Craig back out of his shroud was harder than they expected. First off, the zip on the sleeping bag jammed, then the ground-sheet somehow got twisted and knotted beneath the body, so they actually had to lift and turn his dead-weight over, in order to free it. He slumped back and forth as they moved him, nothing now but clay – cold, ghoulish clay, for his flesh was hideously clammy to touch, and, in the dusky half-light, had turned the colour of bleach.

For all this, it was a futile endeavour. They went through Craig's pockets and searched inside his clothes, even going so far as to strip off his sweater and take down his pants … but though they found a wallet and two spare reels of film for his shattered camera, there was no trace of his mobile phone.

Alan knelt back up, now bathed in chill sweat. 'Not here,' he said simply.

Nug stood. 'Obviously he dropped it when he fell.'

Alan gave him a cynical stare. 'Oh, *obviously!*'

'I hope you're not thinking what I think you're thinking.'

'It's bloody convenient, isn't it?' Alan said.

Nug shook his head. He clearly didn't want to believe what his friend was implying.

Now Alan stood up too. 'Nug. No-one's nicked the sodding satellite phone! You know how expensive that piece of gear is. Don't you think she'd have gone absolutely fucking berserk if it had really gone missing?'

'Any luck?' Professor Mercy asked them from the cave entrance.

They both turned quickly. Her silhouette almost blotted out what little light there was filtering in.

'Er … not much,' Nug said awkwardly. 'We'd better go and check where his body was.'

She considered for a moment, then nodded. 'We'll go through his tent and his rucksack as well. Even if we don't find it, it's no disaster. The boat'll be here the day after tomorrow. I think we can manage for that long.'

And then she was gone, marshalling the others, audibly sending them back to the camp. Nug made to follow her, to Alan's further irritation. '*I'll* wrap him up again, shall I?' he said pointedly.

'Sorry, mate.' Nug came back in to help.

A moment passed as they re-swathed Craig in his groundsheet. When Alan was sure the Professor was out of earshot, he leaned over. 'I thought you were the one who was worried something was going on?' he said quietly.

'It's not *her*, though, is it,' Nug protested. 'I mean, we *know* her.'

'What the hell's got into her, then?'

Nug shrugged, and pulled the sleeping bag up over the corpse's still booted feet. 'Same as has got into everyone else, I suppose.'

'Which is?'

'Grief. Worry.' Nug drew the zip up. 'Look ... she stands to carry the can for this cock-up, *whoever's* fault they decide it is. It's already fucked up the biggest find of her career. She's probably just bottling it all in.'

Neither of them spoke further, but, inside, Alan was in deep distress. He'd long been entranced by Professor Mercy. It wasn't just the fact that every heterosexual male who laid eyes on her wanted to take her to bed, or that she was a dominant figure in her field, with a knowledgeable and charming manner that made her seminars a pleasure to attend; it wasn't just the care and concern she showed, and the fact that she was always there for those to whom she was personal tutor. It was the combination of all these; the blend of professional yet motherly control she exercised over those in her charge. Yet how different things suddenly were now. Alan didn't feel disappointed by her, so much as betrayed … betrayed that she was so interested in her career, betrayed that at the end of the day that meant more to her than the lives of her students, betrayed that this perfect person wasn't as perfect as he'd imagined.

    What other revelations awaited them?, he wondered. At least 32 hours had to pass before they could get off this island. How many other startling stress-cracks would start to show in their fine façade?

ᚠᛁᛏᛘ

The howl was long and low, and it hung on the night air with a mournful resonance.

At first, Alan thought he was dreaming. He *had* been dreaming earlier; dreaming that they weren't camped out on a teeny island just off the northern British coast, but were actually in some vast wilderness of mountains, glaciers and snow-deep pinewoods. How natural that a howl should have sounded in a place like that, but now, as he lay in that vague state between slumber and wakefulness, there came a bustle of movement from the other tents, and a low mumble of voices, and at once he realised that the howl he'd heard hadn't been part of any dream.

Hurriedly, Alan shook himself to clear his head, then glanced at his watch. In the still-pitch dark, the luminous dial told him it was just past two o'clock. He hadn't been asleep that long. By the voices outside, however, the others were clearly up and milling around. He wormed out of his sleeping bag, pulled his boots on and slid from the tent. Various torches had been switched on, which fleetingly had the effect of concentrating the darkness around them, so it was several moments before he was able to recognise who was who.

'I suppose you all heard that, did you?' came a tremulous voice. It was David Thorson. He hadn't yet put his sweater on over his t-shirt, and was hugging himself, either from the cold or from fear. Probably a mixture of both. His normal irreverent humour already looked like a thing of the past.

Alan glanced around, his eyes slowly attuning. Nug was present, looking sleepy and dishevelled, alongside Professor Mercy, who was shining her torch out into the surrounding pines, but finding nothing unusual.

Nug yawned. 'Someone playing stupid games again?' he said.

'Where's Barry Wood?' Alan asked.

Nug shrugged.

'*Here*. Any problem with that?' came a terse reply.

Everyone looked round and saw Barry weaving his way down through the trees on the higher slope. A moment passed, then Linda appeared behind him. She looked a little sheepish. Barry on the other hand was his usual brazen, swaggering self.

'Someone's farting about,' Alan said, biting his lip on what he really wanted to say. 'Don't suppose you know anything about that?'

Barry grinned as he ambled up to the remnants of the fire and warmed his hands. 'Nah ... I've had better things to do.'

Alan glanced at Linda, but she averted her eyes.

Now Professor Mercy came forwards. 'I'm not sure it's a good idea wandering off in the dark. We don't want any more accidents.'

'No problem,' Barry replied. 'Everything's done and dusted, anyway.'

Linda made a move to her tent, but saw that Alan

was still watching her. 'What are *you* looking at?' she asked him.

'Nothing,' he replied, meaningfully.

'Woaa!' David shouted, suddenly bug-eyed. 'Someone's over there! *Who's that?*'

Again, everyone turned, and this time they were transfixed by a humanoid figure, immensely broad and unwieldy, coming slowly and quietly up through the veils of mist hanging over the bog-pools. It was a nightmarish shape, with a burly outline and foggy aura, reminiscent of a hundred cheap and nasty horror movies.

'*Who's that?*' David shouted again, his voice breaking like a prepubescent schoolboy's.

'It's me,' said Clive, suddenly recognisable in the torchlight, and not a little baffled at the panic he'd caused. 'I've been for a pee. That okay?' He was still in the process of zipping himself up.

'You didn't hear anything odd while you were down there, did you?' the Professor asked.

Clive shook his head. 'Such as?'

'A wolf,' David told him.

'Bollocks a wolf,' Alan said, still glaring suspiciously at Barry's broad back. 'It was someone *pretending* to be a wolf.'

'Put the bloody wind up me whatever it was,' David replied.

Clive shrugged. 'I didn't hear anything.'

Everyone pondered this, then Professor Mercy flicked her torch off and moved back towards her tent. 'In that case it's probably a false alarm,' she said. 'It's not as if there aren't plenty of other explanations. For one thing, Craeghatir has been a sanctuary for rare seabirds for quite some time.'

'Yeah,' Alan muttered, 'like poor Craig told us.'

One by one, the others moved back and clambered under canvas. Aside from Alan and Nug, Barry was the last to go. He didn't seem concerned that Linda had already disappeared into her tent without so much as a goodnight kiss. Once the athlete had vanished, Nug turned to Alan.

'You know that was no seabird,' he said.

'I know.'

'So what's going on?'

'Your guess is as good as mine,' Alan replied, though he was now gazing at Barry's tent. Briefly, there was a light on in there, then it was extinguished.

Nug shook his head. 'Why are you trying to pin it on him? I mean, apart from the fact you hate his guts.'

Alan looked at him, surprised. 'He was out there when we heard that howl.'

'So was Linda, so was Clive.'

Alan snorted. 'Linda and Clive aren't tosspots interested in fucking with everyone else's mind.'

'But why would Barry do that? What's he got to gain?'

'I just think he's a prat,' Alan said, 'and that he's capable of doing anything to keep himself amused.'

'And you're absolutely certain your judgement isn't being clouded by ... *something else?*' Nug wondered.

Alan gazed at him hard. 'Whatever *I* think about that goon is irrelevant,' he said. 'Just consider the position, Nug. Someone is fucking around in the wake of a fatal accident. Now, call it moronic insensitivity, call it bad taste, call it silly thoughtlessness. Call it whatever you want, but at the end of the day who do *you* think it's most likely to be?' And with that he went back to his own tent, leaving his pal alone and thinking by the fading glow of the fire.

But sleep wasn't to come easily for the remainder of that night. Despite the emotional drain of the previous day, Alan's brain was now too alert to be closed down. He rolled over and over in his sleeping bag, did everything in his power to relax, but always now his ears were primed for the slightest sound, each one of which caused him to tense up and listen warily. If he heard so much as a flutter of leaves on the breeze, or a snap or pop in the burnt-out embers of the fire, it set his nerves on edge.

As the night wore on, Alan began to feel like a first-time camper. The cold was suddenly getting to him, the dankness was an irritant; he found lumps under his mat which were surely imaginary but which discomforted him nevertheless. His wide-awake eyes constantly scanned the inner nylon skin of the tent for the faintest sign of movement or shadow. Repeated checks with his watch revealed only that the night was slipping steadily past. The first time he looked, it was just past three; the second time it was almost four; the third time it was half past four, and now the pale light of sun-up was infiltrating the camp, the dawn chorus twittering madly in the branches overhead. Still, sleep eluded him.

Sometime between five and six, he gave up on it. He climbed out of his bag again, drew on his boots and went outside. It was another glorious summer morning, the sun already high and throwing dazzling light on the bog-pools, dappling the shady areas under the trees. Nobody else was astir yet, so Alan took a long drink of water, then a leak. After that, it crossed his mind that he might again busy himself clearing the ashes from the night before and preparing another fire. But it was still a little early even for breakfast and, in any case, why should *he* be the one to do all the work?

So thinking, he stuck his hands into his pockets and set off for a walk. He hadn't seen a great deal of the island as yet, and with the death of Craig, it didn't seem like he was going to. Not unless he made a few forays of his own. This seemed like a good time … if any time could be called 'good' in such a predicament.

For several minutes he strolled up through the woods in a vaguely north-westerly direction. Though he could hear the distant *hushing* of the waves, there was a pleasant coastal calm. Blue-green shadows lay between the trees. Alan saw a flash of red as a squirrel scampered along a low bough. At length, however, the trees thinned and he found himself at the head of a gorge or ravine lying between high granite bluffs. It was narrow – perhaps 20 yards across at the most – and deep in lush grasses and fallen stones. It ran in a reasonably straight line for about a quarter of a mile. At the far end of it he could see open hillside and, surmounting that, a tall whitewashed spear-like structure with a glazed section at its top.

The lighthouse.

Alan knew it was private property up there, but he didn't see any harm in taking a look. The building might well be fenced off, in which case his problem would be solved for him, but if it wasn't, what was the harm in a quick mooch about? He set off at an easy pace, hands still in his pockets. As he strode, the sounds of the ocean grew louder, clearer. Now he could hear the crashing of surf, the calling of gulls and gannets.

And then, somewhere close behind him, there was a faint *skitter*, something like a small pebble rolling over rocks.

Alan stopped and turned, but there was nothing and

nobody behind him. In all probability, eroded pieces occasionally fell from the walls of the ravine, while there were almost certainly animals around here too. He'd have thought a remote isle like Craeghatir wouldn't be home to the larger north British mammals, like the wildcat or pine marten, but one never knew. He'd just seen a squirrel, after all. It also seemed highly likely there'd be wild hare around.

He continued on his way, though he had to admit the noise had unnerved him. Despite the warmth of the sun and the mellow feel of the land and sea, Alan was now on edge, distinctly uneasy ... the way a trespasser might feel when he knows he's on somebody else's land and is constantly expecting to be spotted. Even when he emerged from the gorge and found himself way out on a headland with sheer drops to either side, he felt no great relief.

Shaking his head at the curse of his imagination, he progressed up a shallow slope towards the lighthouse and its associated buildings. None of these was fenced off, but all were closed up and wore heavy-duty padlocks on their solid steel doors. On the lighthouse itself, there was a red sign, reading 'DANGER' and painted with streaks of electricity. Alan gazed up. So close, the white-washed signal tower seemed colossal in height. The lowest window in it had to be 20 or 30 feet from the ground. Not that he envisaged trying to get inside for any reason.

He glanced around. In the age of pre-automation, this must have been a desolate post indeed. Having said that, he still found it difficult to shake himself of the conviction that he wasn't alone here. He glanced again towards the high lantern-gallery, to see if someone was up there, gazing back down at him. Of course, nobody was. The feeling lingered, however, even when Alan made his way among the outbuildings; the electricity sub-station, the storage houses, the heli-pad. At length, he moved on past the far perimeter of the complex, and progressed over the final 50 yards of thistle, clover and sea-campion until he reached the tip of the headland. A few feet short of it, he stopped cautiously. He'd just had the brief but chilling sensation that if he went right to the edge, somebody might come sneaking up from behind and push him over. He looked back, but not only was nobody there, nobody could have got within 30 yards of him without his becoming aware of them.

Even with that knowledge it was a dizzying sensation finally to approach the precipice and gaze over it. Cape Wrath, it seemed, was well named, for a spectacular vision of elemental fury now confronted Alan. Some 200 feet below, a bottle-green swell – monumental in size and strength – rose and fell around the jagged black rocks, sending eruptions of surf to phenomenal heights, roaring in the zawns and crannies of the cliffs. Farther out over the tempestuous seascape, the tide drove in via an endless succession of gigantic waves. Here and there among them more shoals of rocks were visible, protruding like teeth through the cascades of foam, creating currents and whirlpools all of their own. These weren't even storm conditions, yet the wind here howled at gale-force, threatening at any moment to pluck Alan from the headland and cast him into infinity, a dust-mote in Nature's blinking eye.

Almost breathless, he finally backed away, turned and staggered towards the station. The very ground had seemed to move beneath his feet back there. It had left him lightheaded.

In comparison, the silent buildings and their aura of

desertion, were strangely homely ... almost comforting. Alan hung around them for a moment longer, wondering just when it was that the manned operation here had ceased, and figuring that it must have been at some point in the mid-1980s – 15 years ago, at least. A long time for a modern structure to be left disowned; though no time at all, of course, in comparison to the Viking barrow. Eventually, he started walking back. A glance at his watch showed that it was now a quarter to seven. Things might be starting to happen in the camp.

He strolled down the ravine at a gentle pace. The sea-wind had dropped remarkably when he'd moved back from the precipice, but down here it was almost non-existent. Overhead, the sun had gone among the clouds, but a still, sultry heat remained. Alan couldn't help thinking that had he been here for a holiday, he couldn't have asked for finer weather. As it was, it might make work on the dig difficult, assuming he could bear to do any. He took his sweater off and tied it around his waist as he walked, mopping sweat from his brow with his forearm.

And then, once again, several pebbles came down from above.

As before, Alan stopped immediately and glanced around. Also as before, the gorge behind him was deserted, but this time he looked up as well. He saw nothing there, but some extra sense was now tingling. He held his ground for a moment, listening. Silent moments passed. Then he heard it: a low, drawn-out snarl; the sound a dog might make when squaring up for a fight.

Alan felt the skin on his neck start to crawl. Perplexed and frightened, he backed away into the middle of the ravine. Just as he did, another stone came bouncing down towards him, this one larger and more jagged. Had it struck him, it might have inflicted injury. Alan didn't wait to see where it had come from. He continued on his way, hurriedly, determined not to panic, though he glanced overhead constantly. The snarling had ceased, but he imagined that whoever – or *whatever* – had made it was now stalking him, following him along the high shelf. Even as the student considered this, more dirt was dislodged from above and came trickling down. There was a further, prolonged snarl, this one more a throaty growl. It was still abreast with him. There was no doubt now; whatever it was, it *was* trailing him.

Alan began to run. Moments later, he was out of the gorge and back among the trees, but the pursuit, he fancied, continued. It sounded as if a heavy body was close behind. Underbrush thrashed, there was a muffled thumping of feet in the heaped pine-needles. The student glanced over his shoulder as he ran, but in his wild, haphazard flight, it was difficult to see anything clearly. Evergreens bounced past, filling his vision, but something *was* back there, coming at speed, following him in leaps and bounds. And now he heard the growling again, hideous and feral, rising steadily in intensity, punctuated by guttural grunts for breath.

Alan's heart was pounding as the adrenaline took over. His lungs were fit to burst, but he charged on all the same. So frantic was he now that he could hardly think straight. He wasn't even sure which direction he was headed in. He began to shout, to scream. Flailing branches tore at his face and body. He darted left and right to avoid tree-trunks, stumbling, staggering, but keeping going. Still it came after him, now howling with animal rage. It couldn't have been more than two or three yards behind. Alan felt that raw, bone-chilling peril that only an unlucky few in life ever experience ... *that death is right behind you, clawing at your collar, its fatal touch terrifyingly imminent.*

Alan gasped for air as he ran, felt the sweat streaming down into his eyes. His lungs exhaled and inhaled in agony. He wanted to plough on, oh how dearly he wanted to plough on, but his strength was ebbing, he was tiring, he wasn't going to make it.

And, more by luck than design, the triangular outlines of the tents hove into view ahead.

With muted sobs of relief, Alan blundered towards them. The sudden smell of wood-smoke was Heaven-sent; the sight of his colleagues moving lazily back and forth – yawning, stretching with the morn – was the finest thing he ever saw. He didn't know whether or not he was still being followed, but he plunged on at full speed.

The others turned questioningly as he finally tottered in among them and fell onto his face, gesturing wildly, stammering as he tried to explain. Even then, at that late stage, he expected something to come and leap onto him from behind, to tear and rend his flesh and clamp its inhuman jaws over the nape of his neck ... so that when someone knelt down and tapped his shoulder, he threw himself over, kicking out, swearing hoarsely.

'Jesus ... Alan!' Nug fell backwards.

'There was something,' Alan blathered, his face red as a lobster, his lips flecked with froth. 'I'm telling you, there was something ...'

He scrambled to his feet and gazed out into the encircling woods. They were still, silent, laced with morning sunlight. Tendrils of mist still hung there, but nothing moved.

'What do you mean, 'something'?' Clive asked. He and the rest approached curiously.

Alan stared around at them. David and Linda looked surprised, Professor Mercy dubious ... perhaps a little sceptical.

'It came after ... it came after me,' Alan added, suddenly acutely aware how bizarre a figure he must be cutting.

'What came after you?' Again, it was Clive who asked the question.

Alan was about to try to explain when there came a sudden movement to the west of the camp. Instinctively, everyone went on their guard. Alan turned madly, gazing into the depths of the trees. Something was approaching, that much was obvious. They heard heavy footfalls, saw branches being pushed aside. There was a loud puffing and blowing; something wasn't just approaching, it was approaching at speed.

'Jesus Christ,' Alan whispered.

He began casting around for a weapon, any kind of weapon. At last he put his hands on a spare tent-pole, and swung it up, ready to brandish it like a club. He wheeled towards the approaching noises ... and, like everyone else, was then nonplussed to see Barry Wood emerge from the trees in shorts, vest and sneakers, coming at a slow, easy trot. The athlete's flesh was pink and gleaming, his blonde hair a wet, tousled mop.

'Morning all,' he said, as he finally reached the camp, slowed up, then commenced a series of stretch exercises.

'Y ... you!' Alan stuttered, approaching him on unsteady feet. *'You bleeding mental case! What did you think you were playing at?'*

Barry looked up, apparently baffled. 'What are you on about?'

'You scared the crap out of me!'

Barry considered this, then shrugged and shouldered his way past. 'Sorry pal. Can't help it if you're a chicken-shit arsehole.'

The athlete was just in the process of taking the water-bottle out of his kit, when Alan grabbed him by the elbow and yanked him about-face.

For tense seconds they eyeballed each other, nose-to-nose. Barry was reacting in his normal aggressive fashion when someone hassled him, though on this occasion he was just slightly surprised at the way his height and breadth didn't seem to be giving him the usual advantage of intimidation; there was also, of course, the not insignificant matter of the tent-pole Alan was wielding. Alan, for his part, was more than ready to fight. Taken to the edge of fear and beyond, a red mist now possessed him ... but even if it hadn't done, with his Lancashire coal-town upbringing, he certainly wasn't going to back off from some Home Counties public school-boy, star rugby union player or not.

Alan muscled right up to the big guy: 'You. Fucking. Wanker.'

'You'd better watch it, bud,' Barry warned.

'Or what?'

'All right, that's enough,' Professor Mercy said, coming between them. The others stepped in and helped, Nug hauling Alan backwards, Linda putting her arms around Barry and glaring at Alan. The two parties separated, though eye-contact remained locked.

The Professor turned to Barry. 'What exactly have you been doing?'

He indicated his sports get-up. 'Jogging. What does it look like?'

'He's a lying sack of shit!' Alan snapped.

'I said enough, Alan!' the Professor shot in. 'And I mean *enough!*'

Another second passed, as she surveyed them both. 'Now look,' she finally said. 'Back off, the pair of you. We've had a shock, a nasty one … but Alan, you're handling it worse than anyone else here. And Barry, you're not helping one way or the other. We've got to get a grip, do you understand? That goes for all of us. We've got to pull ourselves together. We've invested a lot of time and money in this dig, we're not screwing it up by going crazy on each other.'

'He's the one who's screwing it up,' Alan retorted, jabbing at the big athlete with the tent-pole.

'Put that bloody thing down,' the Professor said coldly. 'Right now.'

Grudgingly, Alan threw the item away. His eyes never left Barry's, however.

'Come over here,' said the Professor, beckoning to them both. Sheepishly, rather like chastised schoolboys, they followed her to a spot several yards outside the camp, where she turned to face them again.

'I'm going to have to go back to the mainland tomorrow with Craig,' she said quietly. 'Alan, you'll probably have to come too, as the person who found the body. It may be that the police will want to question all of us. We don't know yet. But the point is this: tomorrow, as soon as *that*, I'll be in a position to turf anyone off this expedition who isn't fitting in. Do you understand?' There was a steeliness about her as she spoke, a tautness in her voice that betrayed real anger underneath. 'Be under no illusions. I *know* why you two are at odds with each other. I'm sure tensions have been heightened by the accident, but I'm damned if I'm going to blow something as important as this find over a teenage-type squabble!'

She paused. They waited in guilty silence.

'That's how the situation stands,' she finally said. 'Another incident like this, and you two are *both* going home.' She paused again. 'Now, is there any chance at all that you might shake hands and make up?'

Barry seemed the keener of the two. He offered his hand first. Alan eventually took it, but only sullenly, with extreme reluctance.

'I still don't know what you were talking about,' the athlete said. 'I've just been jogging, that's all.'

Alan didn't bother to reply. He shook hands, then turned and strode away. This wasn't so much rudeness or defiance on his part, it was determination. Determination not even to contemplate the possibility that it *hadn't* been Barry back there in the woods.

ᛏᛖᚳ

With the semi-fossilised warrior protected by his burial mound, normal stratigraphic procedures were unnecessary. Aside from the dust, time hadn't added its own layers of dirt or topsoil to the interior of the site, animals hadn't disturbed any of the artifacts, there was no danger of contamination of the find by the relics of other periods. Even so, in order to assist in the planned reconstruction of the site back at the lab, before any digging and picking could commence everything had to be carefully measured and photographed. This took up much of the rest of the morning.

Linda laid out the trays and brushes and bags, then prepared her fold-out stool and table, and began sterilising the various tools they'd need in a dish of chemicals. Barry wandered back and forth, writing up the notes of the dig thus far, while Alan, David and Nug put everything on film. This latter task involved shooting the exterior of the barrow with the video-camera, and squirming back inside it with a Polaroid, to take additional snaps of the remains before they were removed.

Professor Mercy, meanwhile, brooded over the engraved serpent on the portal-stone, then went back to the megalith, crouching and re-studying the runes carved there. Alan noticed that she was diverting from her normal methodology. Ordinarily, when puzzling over an inscription, she would first and foremost sketch it out in detail, so that it could be dealt with back at the lab, where source-materials and data-banks might be accessed. Not on this occasion, apparently. She had her sketch-pad and pencils in hand, but no attempt was being made to jot anything down. She seemed determined to try and translate these symbols on the spot.

'She's pretty engrossed,' Alan finally observed.

Clive, who was just about to worm his way back into the barrow, having started to make delicate trips to and fro bringing items out, turned and looked. The Professor was still so busy with her analysis, that she wasn't aware she'd become the object of scrutiny.

'This dig could potentially put her in the history books,' the tutor said. 'I suppose it would be nice for her to find evidence that she's on the right track straight away.'

This made sense, Alan thought. Clive then hunkered down, clambered under the awning and began the complex and fatiguing process of working his immense body through the narrow gap that was the access-tunnel. From inside it, repeated bright flashes indicated that Nug and David were still photographing. Even these were blotted out, however, when Clive finally got in there.

Alan lowered the video-camera, and went and stood beside the Professor. A moment passed, then she glanced up at him. 'Any thoughts?' he wondered.

She still seem preoccupied. 'Er ... not really, no.'

Alan looked again at the uneven lines of writing.

They were facing due-east and, as much of the wind and rain on Craeghatir came from the north and west, only minimal erosion had occurred. The moss and lichens had probably played their own part in preserving the ancient signatures.

'It's pretty well-preserved, isn't it,' he said.

She nodded absently. 'Yes, but it's an idiom I haven't come across before.'

Alan hefted the camera. 'Shall I get a shot of it?'

Oddly, the Professor didn't seem too keen. 'Perhaps later, eh.'

Alan was surprised, but knew better than to question his project-leader. 'What about the portal-stone?'

'Just concentrate on the barrow for the moment,' she said. 'Get it from every angle. Remember to put something in for scale, as well.'

He nodded and went back to what he was doing before. A few moments later, Clive re-emerged from the tomb, looking dusty, puffed and red in the face. The cramped interior was certainly no place for a big man, especially with two of the other guys already inside it.

'I think I'm going for a walk, to get some fresh air,' he said, beating himself down. 'Like the bloody Black Hole of Calcutta in there.'

Alan nodded and smiled. Clive ambled off, checking with the Professor first. She exchanged a few words with him, then stood and came back to the barrow. 'Lunchtime, I think, Alan,' she announced.

Relieved, he switched the camera off. Right on time, David reappeared from the entrance-tunnel, also looking grubby and tired.

'Just the man,' the Professor said. 'Toddle down to the camp, would you, David. Get us a fire going. We'll be cooking in the next 20 minutes.'

The younger student grinned broadly at the mention of food, and, for once without a quip, hurried away to do as he was told, leaving Alan and the Professor standing side by side. There was a moment of silence. Alan glanced round at his mentor. She was lost in thought … by the furrows on her brow, apparently painful thought; by Professor Mercy's normal standards, she was in a very doleful, downbeat mood. He didn't need to be a psychoanalyst to understand why.

'Craig's death *is* a bit of a choker, isn't it,' he finally remarked.

She glanced at him. 'Sorry?'

Alan shook his head. 'No, *I'm* sorry. I made a bit of a scene down there, and I shouldn't have.'

She considered before replying: 'Well … the whole thing's pretty upsetting.'

By now, Barry and Linda had come over to join them. The Professor surveyed them all, her beloved students, and gave them a sad but rather fond smile. 'What's the definition?' she said. 'Ah yes … as I recall, archaeology is supposed to be 'the study of ancient cultures through the excavation and description of their remains'.' She shook her head. 'Despite Indiana Jones' antics, it was never supposed to be dangerous.'

Alan shrugged. 'Like you said, accidents happen.'

'And Craig would go off on his own and do these things, you know, Jo,' Linda put in.

'Yes,' the Professor replied, gazing down the slope into the pinewood.

Clearly their words of consolation were no real solace to her. It struck Alan that he had underestimated the woman at the time they'd found Craig's body; evidently, she felt a deep remorse and guilt about what had happened. Either that or she had something else on her mind that was distressing her more. But *that* had to be nonsense. What could be more distressing for a teacher than the death of one of her star pupils?

'Come on, folks,' the Professor suddenly said, with an attempt at brightness. 'Let's get something to eat.'

There was a mumble of agreement. They called Nug out from the barrow, then set off downhill to the camp. But when they got there, the fire was still not made up, and there was no sign of either David or Clive.

'Now what?' said Barry irritably.

'David's down there.' Linda pointed towards the nearest of the bog-pools.

David was crouching by the water's edge, with his sweater and t-shirt off. He seemed to be washing himself. Alan and the Professor ambled down towards him. David heard them approach and turned. He was dripping wet; arms, face and torso.

'Thought you were making the fire for us?' Alan said.

'Thought I'd scrub up first,' David replied with a grin. 'You know, hygiene? Digging in graves and all that, then cooking lunch.'

'Well your fastidiousness does you credit,' Alan said. 'Now can you get your arse back up to the camp, please? We're all starving.'

David stood and shook his hands dry. 'You mean *I'll* actually get something this time?'

Alan shook his head solemnly. 'Don't push your luck too far, pal ...'

'David?' the Professor said. 'Have you seen Clive?' She was gazing thoughtfully into the trees. Clearly, she hadn't even been listening to the banter.

David shrugged. 'Didn't he say he was going for a

walk or something?'

'I'll find him,' Alan said, moving away.

The professor stopped him. 'It's okay, *I* will. There's something I want to talk to him about.'

And she set off without waiting for an argument. Alan stared after her, puzzled. 'Not like her to do the leg-work,' he finally said.

David chuckled as he pulled his t-shirt back on. 'Hey pal, don't knock it. When the engine driver's willing to do the rubbing-rag's job, you don't hear the rubbing-rag complaining.'

Alan glanced at him with distaste. 'Cool analogy, thanks.'

Five minutes later they were seated around the fire, plastic dishes proffered, while Linda filled the frying pan with cooking-oil, laid several strips of bacon in it, and cracked a couple of eggs on top of them. In essence, she was frying up an omelette, though on other recent field-tips this particular delicacy had come to be known, rather uncharitably, as 'egg-mess'. Not that anyone was complaining. As well as being highly nutritious, Linda's egg-mess was also rather tasty, and quick and easy to throw together. There also tended to be more than enough for everyone, as it was easy to store plenty of fresh eggs and bacon in the cold-box.

'I wonder what Craig did wrong?' David said, as they all sat there eating.

'Get interested in bird watching,' Barry replied.

'You think the police'll come over here, to have a look round?' Linda asked.

Barry shrugged. 'They might.'

'It's pretty cut and dried, though, isn't it?' David said.

Again, Barry shrugged. Alan glanced at Nug,

wondering what *his* view was. Nug remained non-committal.

Linda was about to say something else, when an odd noise broke in from somewhere in the woods behind them. It was like a long, drawn-out *bleat*, though it sounded unnaturally high-pitched, and after they'd been listening to it for several seconds, it was cut off abruptly.

Alan stood up. His face had gone white. 'What the hell was that?' he said.

Barry gave him an irritable look. 'A sheep. What's the big deal?'

Alan didn't hang around to disagree. He dropped his plate, and pounded away into the trees. The others glanced bewilderedly at each other for a moment, then Nug stood up. 'The big deal is, Barry,' he said, *'there're no sheep on this fucking island!'*

Alan wasn't exactly sure where the sound had come from, but he zig-zagged in the general direction, stepping back and forth among the increasingly densely-clustered pines. He was vaguely aware that the others were close behind him, calling his name, telling him to wait up … but he couldn't do that. That sixth sense he'd never previously known he had was tingling again, screaming at him that something terrible had happened, and that he was homing in on the scene of it right now. The apprehension rose up inside him like floodwater. Though he was running as fast as he could, he felt an irrational panic. He had to get there, had to find out what was happening, because he somehow knew it was both evil and unnatural …

Then he entered the glade.

The first thing he saw was the Professor sitting cross-legged, apparently crooning to herself. Then he saw the blood, glistening red among the rich browns and greens. The more he looked, the more there seemed to be of it, and not spattered, but spilled, daubed, thick like tar. And, good God, it was everywhere! On the mounds of fallen pine-needles, on the rocks and cones, running down the bark of the trees, dripping from the nodding heads of the forest orchids.

And then he saw why.

Someone had stripped Clive to his capacious waist. Then they had crucified him. Between two pine trees. Each one of his hands had been fastened to its respective trunk by having a tent peg hammered through it. The torture hadn't ended there, however. He had been crucified back-to-front, and then his back had been brutally attacked.

First the shirt torn away.

Then the flesh.

Then the fat.

Then the bones.

Someone had hacked viciously at the bones, for the rear section of Clive's ribcage now hung apart like two broken, bloodied xylophones. The central ridge of his spinal column was intact and in place, albeit in a vertical line of torn cartilage and jutting white vertebrae, but to either side of it, the moist yellow sacks of his half-deflated lungs bulged outwards through two spectacularly gruesome apertures.

Alan felt as though he'd been hit with a mace. He stood there, swaying, in near paralysis. Beside him, he was vaguely aware of a high-pitched tooting. Seconds seemed to pass before he realised that this was David screaming. A moment later, Barry came up alongside them, and he too began to scream, a dirge of hysterical profanities. The athlete covered his eyes and staggered away, before toppling to the ground. Nug meanwhile, who'd seen death before but never like this, had lurched sideways against Alan, then sank down onto his knees.

'Jesus Christ!' he shouted. 'Jesus Christ Almighty ... *Alan, it's the Blood-Eagle!*'

Alan, still unable to speak, could only nod drunkenly, his eyes riveted on the crimson atrocity, his mouth tight-closed like a clam. He'd known *that* of course, all along. From the first moment he'd set eyes on the eviscerated rib-cage, he'd known ...

The Blood-Eagle. Possibly the most ghastly of all Viking blood-rituals.

In 867, they'd done it to King Aella of York, and in 869 to King Edmund of East Anglia – two sovereigns who fell into Danish hands after their armies were butchered, and who then made the mistake of thinking their royal status would protect them from abuse. Neither, of course, had known at the time about the ferocity of Ivar, his detestation for the 'White Christ' – as his people knew Jesus – and his all-consuming adoration for the Nordic Allfather, Odin, who demanded only quality sacrifices in return for his gifts of rage and lust. Inevitably, on the back of berserk Ivar's five triumphant years on the battlefield, only the gratitude of the Blood-Eagle – the ultimate form of offering – would on these occasions suffice; the slow ruination of the human body with knives and clubs, and the eventual sundering of the rib-cage, so the lungs might be brought out and arranged on the back in the fashion of folded wings, creating a lasting impression of the eagle, Odin's most sacred bird.

Moments seemed to pass, yet Alan was still only vaguely aware of where he was and what he was doing.

From David's direction, he could hear a loud and persistent retching, and the splashing of vomited egg-mess on the forest floor. Hardened though he was to the realities of British history, Alan had rarely had it thrust in his face like this. He now knew that he too was going to vomit. Either that or faint, for his legs suddenly felt like rubber.

'Let's see 'em write this off as an accident ...' he heard Nug mumble.

Then Linda arrived, coming breathless into the clearing, having taken a different route from the rest of them, just to cover all bases. That was very like Linda; she was serious about her martial arts, and prided herself on staying alert and keeping a cool head in a crisis. Of course, up until this moment, she'd never experienced a real crisis, and her immediate reaction now was to let forth a series of wild and piercing shrieks. The eyes looked ready to pop from her head, the veins stood out in her brow. This went on for 30 seconds at least, before she then turned and plunged frantically away into the wood, running pell-mell – to where and for what, nobody knew.

Alan recovered himself sufficiently to go lurching after her, but Linda was fit and strong, and she ran far, far ahead. Minutes passed as he blundered in pursuit, once again tripping, stumbling, whipped by branches. 'Linda!' he shouted. 'Linda, wait!' As far as he knew, she was headed in a vaguely northwards direction, which meant straight towards the sea. In Linda's state, of course, she probably wouldn't be aware of that. '*Linda, Jesus Christ ... Stop!*'

But she wouldn't. Not at first. She dashed blindly on, sidestepping trees with ballet-dancer precision, going under and over branches like she was on an assault course. She'd have stayed well ahead of him all the way, had the horror of what she had just seen not been hampering her, finally to the point where she lost all sense of place and direction. She began to totter and tumble. Her throat was raw with screaming. Her eyes filled up with tears, blurring her vision like fog. She neither saw nor sensed the vast gulf just ahead of her, just beyond the next stand of pines.

'LINDA!' Alan bellowed, running as hard as he could.

She still wasn't hearing him. She went on, sobbing aloud, gasping for breath.

The rush of fresh salt-air hit her in the face. Waves crashed in her ears. It sounded a sudden alarm, but it was too late; her hurtling right foot had now come down in open space. It found no purchase, but went on, down and down. Linda fell after it, suddenly heavy as lead, the world turning upside-down over the top of her ...

And Alan caught her from behind. With a last, despairing lunge, he reached out and grabbed her by the belt of her trousers.

She'd been going so fast that she almost dragged him over but, at the end of the day, Linda weighed about nine stones to Alan's 13 and a half, and he was able to snatch at and take hold of the nearest tussock of vegetation, dig his cleated soles in and stop her in mid-flight.

A strenuous moment passed as he hauled her back over the precipice, then she was on top of him, hugging him desperately, weeping into his shoulder. They sank down to their knees together, still on the very edge of the cliff. Despite the proximity of that, and the perilous experience she'd just had there, Linda was still distraught beyond telling about Clive.

'Oh my God,' was all she could say. *'Oh my God, Alan. Oh my God!'*

'I know, I know,' he said, holding her to him.

'Who ... who could do that?'

'Some maniac, that's all I can think,' he replied.

'Some maniac! Some monster, you mean! Some demented monster! Oh Jesus, his lungs were torn out ...'

'I know.'

Linda laid her head on his chest and began sobbing again. Alan hugged her to him, then glanced down over her shoulder. Far below, the green waves broke on the footings of the cliff with cataclysmic force, geysers of spume hurtling upwards. Farther out, in every direction, the ocean heaved and rolled, bleak vistas of crashing, exploding foam. It was almost primeval. There wasn't another shore in sight, nor even a boat. Alan remembered the Viking skalds, and their references to the so-called 'Poison Sea', the ocean of the apocalypse, filled with great serpents and dead men's ships, all stirring to life as the end of the world drew nigh.

All of a sudden, he became aware of how small and vulnerable he was. The idyllic oneness he'd felt with this wild, forbidding place had long since flown. Behind them, the woods stood dark and silent, though it was still only midday. Watching shadows seemed to creep between the raddled, twisted trunks.

'Linda,' he said quietly, 'we've got to get back. We can't stay here.'

A moment passed, then the girl looked up at him, her eyes red, her beautiful face streaked with tears.

'I mean it,' he said gravely. 'We have to go.'

Slowly it dawned on her what he was saying:

someone had killed Clive, and probably Craig too; almost certainly, that someone was still on the island, biding his time before the next attack. Her expression of grief quickly melded itself into one of fear. She stared nervously into the pinewood, her tears drying, her cheeks visibly paling. Even though, as she had recently so loudly professed, she no longer loved him, she had no hesitation in allowing Alan to lift her to her feet and to hold her close beside him as they made their way back.

Every step of that journey was a nightmare. The open, airy woodland that had previously seemed so tranquil, so picturesque, so typical of the remote Caledonian high country, was now an image of trackless gloom. There was an awesome depth and loneliness to it, a malign stillness in its green and shadowy heart.

'Alan, how're we going to get out of this place?' Linda asked in a small voice.

'The same way we were going to get out before,' he replied. 'The boat's coming back tomorrow. One minute after it gets here, we'll all be on it.'

A twig snapped somewhere behind them. They whirled around like cats ... but saw only the many pillars of the trees.

'Are we even going to last 'til tomorrow?' she wondered, as they strode nervously on.

'Of course we are,' he said. 'There's more than enough of us, if we stick together.'

Two minutes later, though, they were to receive another stunning shock. Neither of them particularly wanted to return to the scene of the killing, but they felt they had no choice. They had to veer in the direction where the others were most likely to be. Before they got back to Clive's body, however, they met Nug. He was still ashen-faced, still shaking with shock.

'You aren't going to believe *this*,' he said, as they approached him.

'What?' Alan asked anxiously.

Nug turned and pointed. They followed his gaze, and saw that, coming idly through the trees towards them, with an almost blissful lack of concern, was Professor Mercy. Surprised, they noticed that she had taken her boots and socks off, and was walking barefoot. White chickweed blooms had for some reason been braided into her flowing blonde tresses.

'Hello there,' she said with a serene smile. 'Have you two got back together again? Oh, that's nice. I'm so glad for you.'

Mummy

They left Clive's body where it was, at first because they were unable to remove it, but later because it made sense to.

Both Alan and Barry tried to loose Clive's hands, but the tent pegs had been hammered in with such brutal strength that they were lodged fast. Then Nug reminded everyone that the police would regard this as a crime scene and, though it was sickening beyond belief to do so, it would probably be for the best to leave the grisly picture untouched. Smeared with blood, shivering with nausea, the two lads withdrew, and the entire party – what remained of it – retreated through the woods to the camp, where they built a much larger fire than normal, then huddled around it in a strained and frightened silence as the night descended.

Professor Mercy was the only one apparently unafraid. She hummed quietly to herself as she sat there, occasionally commenting to the rest on the joys of summer and of camping out under the stars, and all the while linking daisy-chains together and weaving blooms into her hair.

'Who'd have thought it?' said Barry, staring at the woman, visibly spooked. 'She's totally flipped. It's like she's retreated back to her childhood.'

'I'd have thought she'd have been the last one to go,' said Linda, articulating all their feelings.

'That's the value of true love for you,' David commented. 'Enjoy it while it lasts, because when some bugger comes and snatches it away, it'll fuck you up big time.'

Alan, meanwhile, shocked though he was by the Professor's breakdown, could think of little else but the terrible rite of the Blood-Eagle. Even in the endlessly violent world of the Vikings, there were only four or five recorded instances when this most potent sacrifice to Odin had ever been enacted, and most of those were attributable to Ivar, who even by the standards of his own people, was regarded as a deranged beast when the mood was on him. The student couldn't suppress a violent shudder. He turned to Nug, seated next to him.

'Have you ever … I mean *ever*, heard of this in the modern age?'

Nug shook his head dully.

Alan couldn't take it any longer. He leaped up. 'First the Millstone, now the Blood-Eagle. Let's admit it, there's some lunatic on this island thinks he's Ivar Ragnarsson!'

Linda gazed steadily up at him. 'That's impossible. John McEndry's the only boatman in miles. He'd have known if someone else was out here.'

'Perhaps it's one of us, then?' Barry suggested.

Linda gave him a startled look. 'Don't be ridiculous …'

Barry jumped to his feet too. 'Think about it! Who else knows this subject well enough? They don't teach the Blood-Eagle on the National Curriculum, do they?'

The following silence was thick enough to cut with a knife. Only the spitting and snapping of the flames disturbed it. Even Nug, who'd reacted with as much hysteria as anyone else at the first sight of Clive's butchered carcass, but who had probably been the first of them all to get his head back together, seemed uncertain. He glanced warily up at Alan and Barry, as if wondering just how much any of them knew about their fellow students.

Finally, Linda spoke again: 'But why would any of us do it?'

'Perhaps someone's got a bit too wrapped up in this Norse legend bullshit,' Barry said, and he turned and gazed at David. 'Perhaps someone thinks he's *personally* involved.'

David blinked in surprise. 'What're ... what're you looking at me for?'

'Where'd you get that name from?' Barry demanded. 'Thorson?'

David now stood up. He glanced round uneasily. 'My mum and dad...'

'Obviously, but where did they get it from?'

David looked bewildered by the question.

'He means it sounds Scandinavian, David,' Nug said. He too was now watching their youngest member carefully.

'Well ... my great-granddad was from Norway.'

'What a fucking surprise!' said Barry, darkly satisfied.

'Oh come on,' Alan interjected. 'You can't be serious. Look at him, he's just a kid. Whoever did that to Clive had physical strength ... like *you*.'

'Or like *you*!' Linda put in, suddenly standing and pointing. Again, her brief reunion with Alan had ended the moment they'd found themselves back in Barry's company. 'You're not a weakling, Alan.'

It was Barry who replied: 'Yeah, but fortunately for Alan, he was with the rest of us while this happened. And so was I.' He looked again at David, who now seemed very small and isolated. 'You, on the other hand, weren't. In fact, you were also with Craig when *he* got killed.'

David backed away a step. 'This ... this is ridiculous,' he stammered.

But now that he thought about it, Alan began to wonder too. It was true what Barry said: David had been absent from the group during both fatal instances, and on the last occasion, they'd even caught him washing his arms and body.

David started to cry. 'I've not killed anyone,' he insisted, as they advanced on him.

Despite his protestations, they tied him up, not only knotting his hands together, but lashing him to the trunk of one of the nearby pine trees with guy ropes from his tent. He wept and pleaded with them throughout, often piteously, but they felt they had no choice. They stood him in his sleeping bag for protection against the cold before pulling the bonds tight, and told him they'd bring water and food whenever he wanted it, but aside from that, there was little other solace they felt inclined to offer. Barry even suggested looping a limp noose around David's neck and tying it off on one of the higher branches, just to make sure he didn't try to wriggle free during the night, but Nug drew the line at that.

'We're not bloody barbarians, Barry,' he said tersely. 'We're only doing this much because we've no other choice.' And he strode back to the fire.

Barry shrugged, and looked round at Alan. 'Just a precaution. Soon as we're asleep, there'll be nothing between him and us but this lot.' And he reached out and, for the fourth or fifth time, tested the security of the ropes. They were already so taut that he couldn't even get his little finger behind them.

'Try not to enjoy this too much, eh,' Alan advised.

'Like Nug said, we're not barbarians.'

Barry sneered. 'I don't suppose it was barbaric what *he* did to Clive and Craig?'

'We don't *know* it was David,' Alan replied.

'We've a pretty good idea, though, haven't we?' Barry hawked and spat. 'And what's going to happen when we get him back to civilisation? Awww, the poor lad, he's had a terrible upbringing. His dad was a drunk, his sister a junkie, he accidentally saw his mum's stocking-tops at church one Sunday and went round the fucking bend. It's not his fault he did this, he's sick, he's ill. Community care, that's the thing for him.'

And with a bitter snort, he turned and went back to the fire.

'Alan, none of that's true,' David stammered, still tearful.

'I know,' Alan said.

'Surely it's obvious I haven't done any of this! Tell me, how did I get Craig up that tree?'

Alan made no answer. He looked steadily at the boy. The matter of Craig being found 30 feet off the ground was bothering him too, but one thing was undeniable: *someone* put him up there and, so far, David was the only realistic suspect, unlikely though he seemed.

'This is only a temporary arrangement, David,' Alan eventually said.

'How temporary?'

'Til McEndry comes with the boat. Twenty hours,

that's all.'

'*Twenty hours!*' David wept. 'What if I need a piss or something?'

'Piss your pants, like most of us have already done,' Barry shouted from the direction of the fire.

David turned mortified eyes on Alan. 'I ... I can't do that.'

'Don't tempt me, Thorson!' Barry shouted again. 'Or I'll come over there and tie a knot in your dick, as well. That'll solve the problem, eh!'

'Try and get some sleep,' Alan said quietly, before moving away himself.

A moment later, he'd sat down by the fire. The heat and colours of the flames washed over him. Briefly, reality wavered; it was luxurious and dreamy. Then he glanced down at himself, and realised that dry blood still blotched his t-shirt and caked his forearms. Ordinarily, he'd have been repulsed at the very idea, but now – for no good reason he could think of – it didn't concern him sufficiently even to make him get up and go down to the pools, to wash off.

'You know, the berserkers used to deliberately daub that shit all over themselves,' Nug said from across the fire. 'Their hands, their faces, their hair, their beards. Must have been a hellish sight when they were coming at you team-handed.'

He was gazing into the heart of the blaze as he spoke and, fleetingly, Alan saw the same thing: the flames and smoke of a dark and infernal age. He recalled that famous quote from the old English Book of Prayer: '*A furore nordmannorum, libera nos, dominae!*'...'Deliver us, oh Lord, from the wrath of the Northmen!'

It pretty well spoke for itself, of course. The Anglo-Saxons weren't exactly shrinking violets when it came to blood and vengeance, but even they at first quailed in the face of Nordic ferocity. Yet since the 1960s, it had become fashionable in historical circles to rewrite the known facts of the later Dark Ages, and to highlight the positive aspects of Norse culture: their exquisite craftsmanship with wood, metal and stone; their eco-friendly mythologies; their sumptuous writings; their skills as shipbuilders; and their courageous, pioneering spirit. All undeniable, of course – proper analysis of the records revealed the Scandinavians to be farmers and traders at heart, who, when they colonised new land, created flourishing, lawful and artistic communities, and who only occasionally went *a-viking*, as they cheerfully referred to it. Such new thinking often made Alan smile, however. He wondered how the average English or Irish peasant, especially those living by the coast or on the banks of broad rivers, would have responded to that. Whatever the university modernists thought, the written facts held that when the dragon-ships were sighted on the horizon, it was usually very bad news. It meant rape, carnage and destruction on an unparalleled scale. It meant hatred, terror and pain. It meant total war: churches and villages sacked, livestock seized, crops trampled and burned, and a harvest taken of the people; women and children stolen into bondage, men slaughtered, either there on the battlefield, or later, on grim woodland altars, sacrificed to gods that to Christians were more like demonic entities.

And with that latter detail, so often dismissed these days as fiction, Alan felt he was now personally acquainted. It made his guts churn when he thought about it, set his head spinning just to imagine the awfulness of such savage, torturous deaths. Of course, like all Viking sacrifices, the Millstone and Blood-Eagle, as well as having a terrorising psychological role, also served important ritualistic purposes; to grant you the strength of your enemy's spine and the wind of his lungs, respectively. But just because you understood an atrocity didn't mean you could even contemplate condoning it. Surely, only those born in darkness and dire hatred could find it in themselves to spike someone to a tree and turn him inside-out while he still lived?; only those whose deities were forces for utter evil, could bend a man backwards until his spine simply broke, and believe that in doing such a thing to some poor, helpless creature, they would attain power and glory?

The fire suddenly flared, distracting Alan from his thoughts. He glanced up and saw that Barry was throwing more wood into the flames. Like Alan, Barry was also stained with Clive's blood. As the athlete stood there, tall and muscular, black crusty streaks on his arms and t-shirted torso, a determinedly fearless expression on his face, it struck Alan that he no longer felt quite so hostile toward the big guy. The Viking armies who'd tried to enslave England in the 9th and 10th centuries were finally driven into the marshy, eastern portions of the country and forced to sue for peace, because a succession of warlike English kings fought them to a standstill. The likes of Alfred, his son Edward the Elder, and his grandson, Athelstan, responded to the extreme violence of the Norsemen with extreme violence of their own; and, for a time at least, it worked. Bullish and boorish, they and their kind must have been, literally, a royal pain in the arse when you were close to them in the ale-house, but perhaps the warrior class weren't so bad after all. There were certainly worse things in Heaven and Earth than

Barry Wood and his sort.

'You know,' Barry suddenly said, hunkering down, 'I've been thinking. When we get back to the mainland, we can make a mint out of this.'

Alan looked slowly round at him. 'What?'

Barry nodded eagerly. 'We can coin it. I mean, how often do you get stuck on a remote island with a psycho killer? Sunday papers'll be selling their sons and daughters to get their hands on this story.' And, so encouraged, he stood and wandered thoughtfully back to his tent.

A moment passed, then Alan glanced blankly at Nug. 'You know, you think you see something in someone, then ...'

'Don't say it,' Nug replied, shaking his head. 'I know.'

ᛏᛈᛖᛏᚾᛖ

The next morning, David had gone.

A bundle of empty ropes was all that remained by the tree.

'What the fu ...' Nug said, stunned into instant wakefulness.

He'd woken early, and, despite being drowsy and bleary-eyed, had thought first of checking on the prisoner and taking him a bottle of water. Now he turned and staggered away from the bare tree-trunk, shouting at the top of his voice. Within seconds, with the exception of the Professor, who slept on undisturbed, everyone else was up and about. Panic and uncertainty went through them like an infection.

Barry swore and threw his boots on the ground. 'Jesus Christ! I *knew* it was him!'

'We don't *know* it was him,' Alan replied.

'Why's he run off, then?'

'He's probably just frightened. Like I said yesterday, he's only a kid ...'

'He's a guilty bastard!' Barry spat. 'Thank God he didn't do any more of us while we were asleep, that's all I can say!'

Nug was still shaking his head, perplexed. 'I just

don't get it. Those were proper butterfly knots. There's no way he could've untied them.'

Linda, who'd knelt down beside the tree to retrieve the ropes, now turned a pale, frightened face towards him. 'He didn't – *look!*'

And she held up a bunch of rope-stems. Almost to a one, they hung in frayed tatters. Below them, it could be seen that the knots were still intact. Alan approached her incredulously. He took one of the ropes and held it up, rubbing the gnawed remnant between his finger and thumb. It was moist, as though slathered in spittle.

'These … these have been chewed,' he whispered.

The others had now fallen silent. Barry finally came forward. '*Chewed?* They're made of durable nylon! He couldn't have …'

'Well, what else does this indicate?' Alan shouted, thrusting the ragged stub into the athlete's face.

'This is impossible,' Linda said slowly.

Nug turned and gazed up the wooded slope. 'I think we'll get up to the dig,' he said.

Barry stared at him. 'You're thinking of work at a time like this?'

'No,' Nug replied, still gazing uphill, and starting to walk. 'I just think we'd better get up there. Like, *now.*' And he began to run. 'Come on, quickly!'

Without really knowing why, the others followed him. The fear spread through them rapidly. Within seconds, they were virtually racing each other to get there, shouting, screaming, terrified of being left behind.

As he ran with them, Alan found himself wondering about actuality, beginning to contemplate the possibility that this was some prolonged and rather nasty dream. Now that he considered it, it was astonishing the way they had just slid from one world – that sane one where archeologists camped out on Hebridean hillsides and dusted down artifacts all day – into another, a chilling and surreal one – where class jokers became mad killers and six miles of sea was suddenly an unbridgeable void. He hadn't even noticed the point when they'd passed over, where the mundane had ended and the horror had begun. Maybe he'd seen too many splatter movies?; maybe spilled blood and human innards were so ten-a-penny these days that the difference between grim reality and gratuitous special-effect was too negligible for the human subconscious to perceive? Even now, with Alan [CRAIG] and Clive dead, and Professor Mercy withdrawn into fantasy, it was unreal. It was like, at any moment, he expected them all to come out of the woods laughing, taking off their make-up and breaking out the bottles of champagne.

This possibility, no matter how slight, which he clung to precariously over the next few minutes as he trampled uphill, was utterly shattered when they finally reached the top and came alongside the dig ... and found what was left of David.

As below in the camp, the kid had been propped against an upright and securely bound there, only this time the upright was the megalith ... and the bindings were his own entrails.

David's mouth was frozen open in a silent shriek. His eyes were glazed over, and his head lay awkwardly to one side, the mop of ginger hair fluttering in the sea-breeze. All that was visible because his face and head were probably the only parts of his body that weren't sodden with gore. His shirt and sweater had been forcibly removed, and a fissure either cut or torn in his lower belly. From out of this, ravel upon ravel of moist, pink intestine had been extricated, then wreathed tightly around him and fastened solidly in place with a variety of knots equally complex to those that Nug had tied below.

There was a moment of choked silence, during which, incredibly, Alan found himself marvelling that there was sufficient space in the cramped confines of the human abdomen to contain so much tough, fleshy material. Then all hell broke loose.

Linda turned away and began screeching like some bizarre bird; Barry fell into an animal-type crouch, then grabbed up a heavy shovel from the pile of tools and turned savagely on the others; Nug dropped onto all fours and hung his head to the bloody grass. Only Alan stayed where he was. He was appalled, but unsurprised – perhaps because he'd partly expected this, because he'd known all along that David Thorson, no matter how Scandinavian his origins, simply could not be the killer.

Or because he again recognised the depredation for what it was.

The Walk. Another sacrifice to Odin, this one to grant you the courage found in your enemy's guts. Yet again, it was an elaborate speciality of Ivar's. The victim was sliced open, then made to march around a sacred obelisk, unwinding his own bowels as he went, gradually wrapping them around the stone until he either died from shock or haemorrhage, or was hacked down by the watching warriors – though they would show such mercy only in approval of extreme strength or courage. David clearly hadn't made it to that final, more honourable stage.

Linda had stopped screaming, but now was sobbing uncontrollably. She sought Barry's arms, but he pushed her roughly away. 'Just get back, all of you!' he screamed, threatening to swing the shovel. *'Get the fuck back!'*

Nug clambered urgently to his feet. 'Get real, arsehole!' he shouted. 'It isn't possible one of *us* could be doing this. I mean, this is real Dark Ages stuff. We're talking deep-rooted barbarism!'

Barry gave a crazy laugh. 'What, you mean like ... we're too nice?'

'No, he doesn't mean that, but he's right!' Alan put in. 'We've known each other since we started out on our bachelor's. That was six years ago. I'm sure if one of us was twisted enough to be doing this, we'd have sussed them by now.'

There was a tense moment, as they panted and sweated and stared each other down.

'So w ... what are we saying?' Barry finally stammered. 'There *is* someone else on this island, after all?'

Alan nodded, breathless. 'Someone who's been watching us all the time we've been here.'

Linda whimpered as she glanced over her shoulder. The others did the same; it was unavoidable. The steep pinewoods below them now took on a dread aspect. The dim spaces between the trees were suddenly deep, impenetrable; the calling of gulls, which had previously echoed along the cliffs, was now uncannily silent.

'Right,' said Nug resolutely. 'We stick together for what's left of the time we're here. And we stay up on this hill. It's exposed, and if we keep vigilant, no-one should be able to sneak up on us.'

Barry nodded, then bent down, scooped up the pick and handed it to Linda. 'Anyone who hasn't got a weapon had better make sure they get one,' he said, hefting the shovel like it was a halberd.

Nug picked up a trowl. Alan went for the hand-axe ... then froze rigid.

'Oh shiiit,' he said slowly. He glanced up at them all with haunted eyes. 'The Professor. She's still down there. And she's on her own!'

Thirteen

The Professor was okay. In fact, she was thoroughly enjoying herself.

She was now stark naked, and lay full length on the ground just to one side of the camp. Her arms and legs were spread, and she'd festooned her entire voluptuous body with daisy chains. She was humming gently, her eyes riveted on the daylight glinting through the high branches.

They stood for a moment, watching her. Then Barry snorted. 'This is almost getting comical,' he said.

Linda hurried up and helped the Professor to her feet, quickly stripping off her own plastic cagoule and draping it over her shoulders. It covered the woman to just below her naked buttocks.

'Any other time you saw the Prof dressed like that, you'd want to scoot to the bog for a quick one off the wrist, wouldn't you,' Barry added. 'Now that'd feel like a sex crime.'

Nug mumbled in agreement. Alan's thoughts were elsewhere, however. 'Listen,' he said, 'about this plan to just stay on the defensive. I've been thinking … I mean, I'm in favour and all that, but why don't we check out the lighthouse first?'

Initially both Nug and Barry were too distracted by the sight of Linda ushering the now-giggling Professor away into the shelter of the camp, to respond. When they finally did, Nug was puzzled: 'The lighthouse? What's the point? Didn't you say it was all locked up?'

Alan nodded. 'Yeah, but if we can break in somehow ... Well, there might be some communications equipment.'

'You mean like a radio?' said Barry.

'Or even a phone,' Alan replied. 'I mean, no-one's stationed there, but people will have to come and do maintenance now and then. There might even be stuff left over from when it *was* manned.'

Nug and Barry looked warily at each other. Though they were loathe to admit it – a trek up to the island's remote north-western tip was likely to be an ordeal and a half under these circumstances – both clearly felt it would be worth a try.

'So are we *all* going?' Linda asked, when Nug had finished explaining the plan.

Alan shook his head. 'No. We're doing what we said we were doing. I suggest you, Nug and ...' He glanced at the Professor, who had now been talked into pulling on some waterproof leggings; she smiled back at him, a little girl lost in a world of wonders. 'You, Nug and Jo, make your way back up to the barrow. That way, you should have a good view of the island's interior, and at the same time can look out for passing boats, if there are any. You see one, you holler yourself hoarse. Light a fire or something.'

Nug nodded, and felt at the zipped pocket in his khaki pants, where on field-trips he always kept a box of matches.

'Me and Barry'll go and check out the lighthouse,'

Alan added.

'Why you two?' Linda asked.

They looked at her. She was watching Alan with a mixture of suspicion and fear. Like the rest of them, she was now pale, worn, bedraggled with dust and sweat. Her fists were clenched so tightly around the rubber-clad handle of the pick, that her knuckles glowed white.

'I mean ... no disrespect to Nug,' she added, 'but I'd rather have Barry with me.'

Nug shrugged. Alan however shook his head. 'If I'm right about the radio, anyone going to the lighthouse is likely to draw this lunatic out. They're almost certain to get attacked first, because he can't afford to let them reach it.' He stared at Linda. 'So ... you may prefer to have Barry, but the chances are I'll *need* him.'

Linda returned the stare boldly, unimpressed by his self-sacrifice. Beside him, Alan felt Barry stiffen. 'So we're going as bait?' the rugby player said.

'Something like that.'

'Nice of you to tell me.'

Alan rubbed his forehead. He was too tired to argue further.

'And if you two are both killed, what happens to us?' Linda asked.

'We do what we said,' Nug told her. 'Stay around the barrow and form a defensive position. If the worst comes to the worst, we'll have only six hours to wait before McEndry gets here.'

There was a silence as they considered this possible, rather awful outcome. Six hours wasn't so long in the real world, but *here*?

'Any more questions?' Alan said. There weren't any. He glanced skywards. The sun had long ago vanished under a cover of heavy clouds, but a simmering summer heat had now descended on the island. He didn't want to say it, but it looked as though a storm was brewing.

'Let's get a move on,' he finally muttered. 'I can't see there's anything to be gained from hanging around.'

'Clive'd probably agree with you,' said Barry, as the two of them set off across the low valley, circling the bog-pools and trudging up through the woods towards the ravine.

Five minutes later they'd entered it, but from here on the going became slow and cautious. Alan had drawn the hand-axe from his belt and was now nervously scanning the high places above them. No faces peered down, however; the only sound was the scuff and scrape of their boots on the stones ... that and the faint, eerie echo it created.

'If we do manage to get into the lighthouse, we'll give it a good going-over while we're there,' Alan said. 'Search it all the way up, from its basement to its the lantern gallery. Be a good place for someone to hide out.'

Barry gave a grudging grunt. 'You seem to be giving a lot of orders at the moment.'

Alan glanced sidelong at him. 'Why ... do you think *you* should be?'

'That's a stupid idea, is it?'

'Get a life, Barry.'

The athlete scowled. 'I know you've still got the hots for Linda, you know.'

'You really want to talk about that now?'

Barry smiled to himself. 'There's nothing to talk about. She's with me. That's all there is to it. You're like ... totally out of the picture. If you were ever even in it.'

Alan found himself coming to a standstill. There was

a tingling along his spine, a sudden singing in his veins. It wasn't a sensation he'd ever had before, but he liked it. A powerful, throbbing heat seethed through him.

It wasn't like it was his own hand, when he reached out and grabbed Barry's shoulder ...

The next thing Alan knew, he was gazing dreamily up at the sky. It was framed between the rock walls of the gorge; as he gazed at it, two white seabirds flitted across. From far away came the gentle lulling of the waves. The breeze whispered in the spikes of heather next to his head.

And then the screaming started. The terrible, terrible screaming. It began like a whimper, like a sound of confusion or bewilderment. But it rapidly grew in volume and intensity, until it banged around inside Alan's skull in a deafening, hysterical frenzy.

Perplexed, he turned his head to look. And that was when he saw Linda, backing slowly out of his vision, her facial expression like one of those Greek drama masks, the gaping mouth fixed in a rigid shriek, the eyes ready to start from their sockets, they were so wide and manic.

Alan was utterly lost for words. He knew things had been hard between them recently, but what was all this shit about? He tried to talk, but couldn't. For some reason he lacked the strength. Not that it mattered much. Linda was already out of earshot. In fact, a moment later, she was out of view. She'd stumbled backwards away from him, until he could no longer see her. He then heard what he assumed was the fading hammer of her boot-soles as she turned and fled properly.

Alan wondered what he'd done this time to annoy her. Then he wondered what he'd been doing, full-stop.

Why the fuck was he in this position? It had suddenly struck him that he was flat on his back, and that his body, which he was only vaguely aware of, felt so relaxed that he could barely move it. He tried to remember what had happened, but his memory came back only in spits and spots. A ship's prow rising and falling; a long green shore. Then, like a dash of cold water, he recalled the deaths of Craig, Clive and David, and a bolt of horror went through him.

He tensed where he lay. The word 'Barry' came to his lips.

Barry ... yes. Barry must have hit him, or something ... knocked him unconscious, though Alan had no actual recollection of that. He knew that something angry had passed between them. Yet, when he turned his head sideways, he felt no dizziness, no pain, no stiffness in his neck or shoulders. If anything, he felt good, refreshed, as though he was re-emerging from a long, restful sleep. Apart from one thing, of course. The fact that he was wet all over.

Drenched.

Now Alan sat up and gazed down at himself ... and for a moment, his mind went blank with shock.

It was as though someone had brushed bright red paint all the way up the front of his trousers and shirt. His boots were coated as well, and his arms and hands. They literally were *coated*, front and back, as though they had actually been dipped in the paint.

Except that, it wasn't paint.

Alan realised that much even before he staggered upright, his stomach churning in on itself, a hot, metallic reek now breaching his nostrils. He turned where he stood, viewing the ground around him. Red too. Bright red. In fact, there was red everywhere, streaking the heather, spattering the boulders, daubed in vivid filigrees on the rugged walls of the canyon, dripping from mossy overhangs, forming thickening rivulets between the smaller stones and pebbles.

Some atrocity had been enacted here. Some minor holocaust.

Or perhaps not so minor.

For when Alan finally turned 180 degrees and surveyed the ground directly behind him, his heart almost stopped in his chest.

Barry lay there. What had once been Barry. A parody of Barry. A sick joke of a thing formerly known as Barry. And incredibly, it still lived.

Alan approached on faltering feet, over ground awash with the blood still pumping from the hacked and jagged stumps where the naked athlete's arms and legs had once been attached, still spouting from the ripped, raw hole in his face where his braggart's tongue used to dwell.

Even then, deranged as it no doubt was, unable to focus on anything but its own mind-numbing torment, the blasphemous ruin of a man tried to shuffle away, feebly, pathetically, able only to use the muscles in its buttocks and its back, the severed ends of its truncated limbs twitching, the eyes rolling in terror in its tortured face.

Alan reached a shaking, helpless hand towards his former foe. His own strength was ebbing, however, his own head swimming with nausea. Finally he turned and fell onto his stomach, retching violently, wave after wave of slime and mucous rushing from his mouth.

Even as he lay there vomiting, he beheld new horrors: perhaps 10 yards away was a wide flat rock, now riven with multiple slash and chop-marks, and of course splattered deepest crimson. Beside it lay countless slivers of meat and bone, muscle and gristle. Strong, supple, athletic limbs now so much mulch and mince; and, beside all that, the hand-axe – bright red from the edge of its shiny blade to the base of its hickory handle – that had been used to render even the renderings, to ensure that all the miracles of modern science could never make good this mutilation.

It was no consolation to Alan to know where this latest madness had come from, to recall the hideous moments in the old chronicles when Viking raiders were said to have left mockeries of men in their wake; pitiful half-creatures, no longer able to plough or hoe, to thresh, to sow, no longer able even to feed themselves, to attend to their own toilet, to climb from their beds in the morning; tiresome lifelong burdens for the families they'd better hope would be prepared to look after them. And, of course, Ivar, notoriously associated with this cruelest of butcheries. Ivar again. Always *IVAR!*

Alan now hated the infamous name more than any other in history. More than Hitler, Stalin, Vlad the Impaler, Jack the Ripper! He called curses down upon it as he clambered to his feet, grabbed up the axe and tottered back to where Barry lay, the lips blue on the cripple's twisted, rictal mouth, the eyes still rolling, yellow like marbles, the pupils startled, permanently wide.

Alan couldn't stand any more. Screaming aloud that he hoped Ivar the Boneless was burning in the deepest tract of Hell, he drew the axe back over his shoulder, then swung it down with every ounce of strength he had, driving it inches-deep into the front of Barry Wood's skull, splitting him open between the eyes, and ending the poor wretch's agony in a single murderous blow. Instantly, those eyes glazed over. Fresh blood spurted from the gruesome new wound, but only for a matter of seconds, at the end of which it slowed to a gentle, gurgling trickle.

Jesus God Almighty, it was no wonder Linda had run. In fact, the next thing he knew, Alan was running himself. Stupored, he lurched down the gorge towards the woods, the hatchet swinging limply from his hand. Torrid moments passed as he stumbled through the trees, the summer heat seeping into him, his pallid flesh crusting over as the blood congealed, his clothes hanging in thick, clotted folds. Sobbing for breath, he blundered from one trunk to another, all the time gibbering, choking, calling out for help, suddenly heedless that his cries might bring the ruthless slayer down on his own head.

When he finally toppled into the camp, there was nobody there; the fire was a heap of ashes, the tents unattended. Without thinking, he turned and began lumbering uphill in the direction of the barrow. That's where Nug had said they'd be, holding out on the most exposed portion of the island, watching all flanks at the same time.

For this reason, they saw him long before he reached them.

Nug had just been in the process of cutting David's stiffening body down from the megalith, sawing through the taut coils of pale, slippery intestine with the edge of his trowl. Linda was now beside him, however, jabbering insanely, gesturing wildly with the pick. In contrast, and in near-surreal fashion, Professor Mercy was further down the slope from the other two, collecting more flowers. As Alan hobbled towards her, spittle dripping from his bloodied chin, she looked up and gave him a joyful, child-like smile ... which lasted for less than perhaps five seconds, by which time she had registered the state he was in, the desperate, monstrous expression on his face, and the terrible weapon clasped in his crimson claw. With at first a whine of fear, then a wail, then finally a prolonged shriek of utter, abject terror, the woman turned and fled, throwing herself down the hill and scrambling away into the pines, her screams echoing and echoing long after she'd vanished from view.

Alan tried to tell her not to go, tried to totter after her, but his strength had left him. As the other two came down the slope towards him, angry, frightened looks on their haunted faces, he sank weakly to his knees, regarding them bug-eyed, slack-jawed.

'A ... Alan,' Nug stuttered, also falling to his knees. 'What the fuck ... ?'

Linda was more demonstrative. *'You son of a bitch!'* she screamed, dashing up to Alan and smashing him on the side of the neck with the side of the pick.

'Wait ...' he gasped, falling sideways into the grass. 'Wait ...'

She raised the pick over her head, and it seemed for one moment that she genuinely intended to bring it down, to impale her former lover with it. She probably would have done if Nug hadn't suddenly thrown himself onto her, dragging her backwards. She screeched and swore and kicked, but as she did Alan managed to explain what had happened. At least, the little of it that he could. He stammered out what he knew; about his blackout, about the horrific wounding of Barry, about the fact that their own hand-axe had been used to do it ...

'And you saw no-one?' said Nug, repelled by the grisly tale, but also astonished that Alan had emerged unscathed.

Alan shook his head, dazed.

Linda wasn't convinced. She tried to leap at him again. '*You* did it! I know you did!'

Again, Nug had to restrain her. All Alan could do was shake his head.

'Alan, this might be a crazy question,' said Nug, 'but you're absolutely sure *you* didn't do it?'

'What ... what the hell do you mean?'

'Look at the state of you, man! I mean, you were covered in blood before, but not like this!'

Alan shrugged. 'But I was right next to him, I was rolling in it ...'

'And you don't remember what happened?'

'How could I? I was out. I must've been hit from behind ...'

'You murdering bastard!' Linda spat. 'You've hated Barry ever since I started seeing him!'

Alan gazed at her. 'Are you nuts? I wouldn't chop him up into dog-food, would I!'

'It's him, Nug!' the girl insisted. 'You wanted to know who the killer was, well now you do.'

Only slowly was it beginning to dawn on Alan what she was actually saying. 'Linda ... for fuck's sake! I was with you all the other times, wasn't I?'

And that, of course, was true. Stubbornly, though, Linda refused to believe it. 'He's in on it, then. He must be ...'

Rage finally breaking through, Alan jumped back to his feet and began gesticulating with the axe. 'You stupid bitch! Aren't you listening to what I'm telling you!'

'Put the hatchet down, Alan,' said Nug, watching the blade carefully.

Alan rounded on him. 'You think it was me, too?'

'All I'm saying is ...'

'How long have we known each other?'

'Just put the hatchet down and we'll talk about it.'

Alan looked hard at him for a moment, then came to his senses. With a shrug, he laid the axe on the grass and stepped back. 'Okay ... it's down.'

Linda promptly snatched it up. 'Murdering bastard!' she again snarled.

'It wasn't me,' he maintained.

'I think it was, Alan,' said Nug slowly.

'Nug ... you know I'm not a murderer!'

'I know *you're* not,' Nug replied. 'It's what got into you that is.'

There was a moment of silence. Linda stared round at him, nonplussed. 'What're you talking about?'

'You've got to listen to me, both of you. You've got to hear me out.' Nug shook his head and held out his hands, as though he himself wasn't entirely convinced by what he was going to say. His nut-brown face set in a tight frown. 'I think ... I think Jo worked this out earlier ... I think it's been on her mind for quite a while. You wanted to know what helped flip the coolest, toughest mind among us, apart from the loss of her boyfriend? Well now I'm going to tell you. And it's going to take some believing.'

He paused, looking from one to the other. Alan indicated that he should continue.

So he did: 'Ivar was a berserker, right. That means, according to Nordic belief, his soul was harnessed to the wolf-spirit. In times of anger, the wolf took over. It made a guy who was already mad, bad and dangerous to know, into a virtual monster! He was unstoppable in battle, he showed no mercy to his prisoners. He tortured and killed them horribly, because that was the way of the feral spirit that controlled him ...'

'It's a bloody myth, Nigel,' Linda reminded him.

He shook his head vigorously, a frenzy of sweat and hair. 'No it isn't! Not entirely. Listen to me ... The traditional funeral for a Viking overlord involved cremation, usually in his own longship. We *know* that to be true. So I ask you, why the hell was Ivar buried and not burned?'

'What are you saying?' Alan ventured to ask. 'That they were frightened of the wolf-spirit?'

'Of course they were!' Nug grew visibly more agitated as he expounded his theory. 'Listen. We've read enough of the sagas to know the berserkers were of great use to Viking leaders in war-time, but they also terrified the shit out of them. They didn't want too many of those guys knocking around. What kind of instability would that have caused in a militarist society based on loyalty and blood-ties?'

'And your point is?' Linda wondered.

'Jesus, isn't it obvious? If Ivar was cremated, the wolf-spirit would have been freed to wander, to cause death and mayhem. Just like it's doing here.'

She was now gazing at him as if he was someone she didn't know. 'Are you serious?'

'Well what do *you* think's been going on?' Nug gestured around them, at the woods and hillside, at the vast northern sky. 'Look at this place. It's in the middle of nowhere. There's no-one else here committing these murders, Linda. We've been doing it to each other. Alan's just killed Barry, like Barry killed David, like David killed Craig and Clive. But none of them remembers it, because it wasn't really them. It was Ivar's wolf.'

'Nug,' Alan said slowly, 'even assuming your theory's correct, it can't be Ivar's wolf. Like you said, Ivar wasn't cremated. The wolf should still be trapped in his rotting bones.'

Nug shook his head. His expression darkened. 'I don't think it works like that. They didn't just find a deserted island and entomb Ivar on it, Alan. They sealed him in with rune-magic. You saw that carving on the portal-stone. That was some kind of holding spell, just like the gods invoked on Loki. And now we've gone and broken it.'

'It's out then,' Alan said.

Nug gave him a bleak stare. 'We've got four dead bodies, all killed in Viking rituals. Backbone, lungs, guts and now the limbs as well. Christ, what more evidence do you need?'

This too was beginning to make sense to Alan. 'You're saying he's rebuilding himself?'

'Only on a spiritual level. In the manner his gods demand, in payment for his power.'

'As a result of which, you're saying that he, Ivar, this *thing*, can just possess any one of us at any time?'

Nug rubbed his brow. 'It's all supposition. But ... yeah. I think so.'

Alan glanced round uneasily. With the thickening cloud cover, long deep shadows lay among the trees. A gloom was even settling over the ridge above them.

'I doubt you'll see him ... *it*,' Nug added. 'It's a ghost. It has no substance.'

'Yeah ... right,' said Linda, with a choked laugh. 'Very convenient.'

Nug glanced round at her. 'It's hard to believe, I

must admit.'

'It's bloody impossible to believe,' she retorted, taking a step away from them. 'But while you're trying, I'm going to find the Professor.' She hefted the axe and pick. 'Either one of you two fucks comes after me, and you'll get these in your cranium.'

'Come on, Linda,' Alan protested.

'Come on, nothing!' she snapped. *'Ghosts, wolf-spirits* ... *Jesus!* This is murder, pure and simple. Some nut-job's finally come out in his true colours. There's only us three left, and I know it isn't me. Therefore, it's one of you two. And *you*, Alan, are favourite. So keep your fucking distance, and I mean it.'

And with that she'd gone, hurrying down the slope and slipping out of sight into the trees. Alan looked wearily at Nug. 'We'd better go after her.'

Nug nodded and, together, they set off in pursuit. In a short while, they'd come to the camp. It was still deserted, though a couple of tent-flaps had been thrown up as though Linda had been here, searching for the Professor. Then came the sound of a voice, a female voice, down by the bog-pools.

The two men set off again. When they reached the water's edge, they saw the women close to the far side. Professor Mercy had removed her waterproofs and waded out naked into the pool until she was waist-deep; now she stood there, arms outstretched as though crucified, her wet blonde hair streaked down over her breasts. A number of water-lilies floated around her in a ring. As before, she seemed to have sought to encircle herself with natural beauty, providing an illusory defence against the horrible reality of what was happening. If so, it was evidently working, for she seemed totally oblivious to Linda now coming into the water behind her, speaking softly, telling her that everything was going to be alright.

And only then did it strike Alan, *really* strike him, that Nug's incredible thesis might very well be correct. Okay, Professor Mercy had lost Clive in an unimaginably awful fashion, but she had always been so strong, so stable, a reliable rock in the whirlpool of university life, and an unchallenged expert in her field. But perhaps that deep knowledge, that clarity of vision had worked against her? For surely only a revelation of staggering horror – magnified a thousand-fold by the untimely loss of her love in the midst of it – could have done this?

And as though in direct response to Alan's thoughts, the Professor seemed to come awake. She turned slowly, arms still outspread, and locked eyes with the younger woman, who had now almost reached her. For a moment there was a smile of understanding between them – a brief telepathic pow-wow, sister to sister – then Professor Mercy broke down.

Weeping piteously, she fell to her knees, coming almost to the depth of her neck in the water. Even then she toppled forwards slightly, so that her head came to rest on Linda's hip. The student looked taken aback, but responded in kind, embracing the older woman, brushing her sodden hair into the nape of her neck.

Nug glanced awkwardly at Alan. 'Maybe we should keep our distance?' he said. 'I mean, watch them and all that, but ... you know, not get close enough to freak them out.'

But Alan wasn't hearing him. 'Why's she taken her clothes off again?' he wondered aloud.

Nug looked back. Again, Linda had helped Professor Mercy to her feet, though the two women were still in a clinch. In fact, they seemed to be getting into *more* of a clinch as the men watched. Initially, the professor was hugging the girl for all she was worth. Then, suddenly, she locked one arm behind her neck. Linda at first tried gently to resist; then she began to struggle; then she began to shout. But the Professor was stronger; literally overpowering. When she clamped her mouth over Linda's, and thrust one hand under her sweater to paw at the breasts beneath, there was almost nothing the younger woman could do about it.

Alan and Nug stared, aghast. At first they were too stupefied to react, so for several seconds longer Linda fought alone. She scratched and bit, did everything the steely grip allowed her. But to no avail. Only when the Professor grabbed down at her crotch, grasping it mercilessly, was the stranglehold broken. Linda tried to go into her martial arts routine. She hit the Professor with blow after blow, but none of it meant anything compared to the crushing pain between her legs. She twisted and gave a muffled scream of agony.

The Professor responded by lifting her mouth from Linda's, and laughing dementedly. Then, with seemingly no effort at all, she took the girl by the throat as well as the crotch and raised her bodily from the water, lifting her up until she was high over head and throwing her.

Almost impossibly, Linda travelled several yards through the air before crashing into the muddy shallows by the shore. Her assailant wasn't finished there, however. She stalked in pursuit of the winded, gasping girl, reaching down and hauling a heavy, nobbled branch from under the lily-pads as she went.

The two men had now started into the water. Frantically, they shouted warnings. But Linda was too stunned to make sense of them. She looked up groggily, and only realised the Professor had a weapon when she saw it arcing through the air towards her. She tried to shield herself with one arm, but it made no difference. The arm was smitten down, and the sodden wood impacted on the girl's skull, cracking across its middle.

Nug screamed profanities as he tried to get there, but both his and Alan's progress was slowing dramatically; they were now waist-deep, and their feet were sinking in semi-liquid muck.

Stunned by the blow, Linda slumped down onto her face. With a shriek of insane glee, Professor Mercy struck at her a second time. Again, the wood collided with the girl's already bloodied head, this time smashing itself in two. Linda rolled sideways in the mud. It didn't halt the attack. The Professor now commenced beating the girl up and down her prone body, using both pieces of the broken club like unwieldy drum-sticks.

'Believe me now?' Nug gasped, as the two men fought their way across.

Alan watched transfixed as he struggled on, never having seen such ferocity in a physical assault. Not happy, it seemed, with the two cudgels, the Professor now began stamping on Linda with her bare feet, paying yet more attention to her head, which lolled limply from side to side as it was kicked and buffeted.

'You mad, barbaric bastard!' Alan screamed, finally realising that, whatever was going on on this hellish island, this was *not* Professor Mercy he was watching.

She, he ... *it*, turned to face them and, rather than fleeing from the superior odds, gave a long, crowing ululation, then hurled itself forwards. The men were still knee-deep, but the possessed woman came at them with the strength and energy of a race-horse, her face a contorted mask. The blows she rained down on them were vicious. One made jarring contact with Alan's shoulder, and for a moment he felt certain it was broken. Another ripped across Nug's left cheek, laying it bare to the bone. They grappled with her, trying at first to restrain her, but so fiercely did she resist that this rapidly became a futile course. Soon Alan was hacking punches into her body, while Nug had wrapped his brawny arms around her neck and was trying to drag her down into the frothing water. When the pieces of wood were wrested from her grasp, she tore at the men with her fingernails, slashed at them with her teeth. Her strength seemed superhuman. She drove a knee into Alan's groin, knocking the wind out of him with a single blow, then turned and butted Nug full in the face, smashing his nose nearly flat. As he squawked and staggered backwards, fresh blood pumping through his clasping fingers, she rent at the ribs exposed through the tears in his t-shirt, flaying flesh from the bones.

This wasn't so much a fight as stand-up butchery, Alan realised. Professor Mercy ... Ivar ... whatever this monstrous thing was, was tearing them apart while they were still alive.

He clambered to his feet and threw himself onto her from behind. She twisted and went down on one knee, tossing him over her shoulder like he was a sack of feathers. He'd been ready for this manoeuvre, however, and as she threw him, he snatched handfuls of her long blonde hair so that when he splashed down, he was able to drag her head after him and plunge her face beneath the foaming surface. She still fought wildly, hammering blows into him. Nug, however, was sufficiently recovered to fling himself on top of her as well, and now, strength combined, they were able to force the raving woman entirely under the water, and to hold her there.

Seconds seemed like minutes as she writhed beneath them, as they fought to keep her down with everything they had. It scarcely occurred to them that what they were actually doing was drowning someone. So vicious had the attack upon them been that they'd instinctively moved from mastery to murder as a solution, and they weren't even conscious of it.

But it was more difficult than they'd ever imagined, mainly because both of them were now utterly exhausted. Even when the Professor ceased struggling, she proved a killing weight to lug across the pool; her splayed limbs had tangled themselves in pond-weed, her entire naked body was plastered in mud.

'Is ... she dead?' Alan stammered.

'Dunno,' Nug gasped. 'I'm no expert ...' He was grey-faced with pain. Blood leaked profusely from his broken nose, from the countless slashes and gashes on his neck and torso.

Five minutes later, they'd dragged the limp woman out of the water and were hauling her by the feet up through the woods, the twigs and pine-needles slithering around her, her golden hair streaking out behind.

'What the hell are we doing this for?' Alan wondered. He too was racked with pain.

'Got to get her up to the dig,' Nug replied. 'Enclose her in the barrow and block it up again.'

Alan gazed at him. 'You sure that'll work?'

Nug shook his grizzled head, his sodden hair flopping about. 'No idea. We'll stuff all the relics back inside as well, Ivar's bones, everything ...'

It took them over a quarter of an hour to pull the woman up through the pinewoods and out onto the open hillside. At no point did she speak or even stir. Her face remained deathly white, the now bruised and broken features as composed as though she was asleep.

'I can't believe we're doing this,' Alan panted.

'You got any better ideas?' Nug replied.

'God help us. If she isn't dead, we're talking about burying her alive!'

Nug said nothing for a moment, but progressed slowly up the slope, wincing with pain. 'At the most, it'll be for a few hours,' he finally muttered. 'The sooner we get to the mainland, the sooner we can get someone back here to try and sort this bleeding mess out.'

At last they got alongside the barrow. Both men sank to their knees, wheezing for breath.

Above them, the sky had turned a sombre slate-grey. The wind gusting past was still seasonably warm, but growing progressively stronger and louder. It was as though the whole atmosphere of the island was slowly, subtly changing. Up on this exposed and blasted piece of hilltop, it was difficult to picture the peaceful, sun-laced pinewood they'd been camped in for that last couple of days.

'Come on,' Nug said, stirring himself to life again.

They hauled the Professor over to the entrance passage. Nug went in first, backwards, dragging the woman by her arms. Alan followed, pushing, shoving, doing anything he could. They had no torch with them now, of course, so it was pitch-black in there. They were no longer concerned about the niceties of archaeology, however. If valuable things crunched and broke under their knees, they felt it was a price worth paying. They didn't try to arrange Professor Mercy's body so that it wouldn't interfere with the find; they simply dumped her in the interior, then scrambled back outside, one after the other.

Nug went straight to the field-lab, knocked the awning aside and grabbed up handfuls of those relics they'd so far brought out. 'Get as much as you can,' he said, hurrying back to the barrow.

Alan did, and for several minutes, they crawled in and out of the tomb, re-depositing everything they'd found. The corroded helmet, the coat of mail, the fragments of skull and rib, the brooches, the book-mounts, the pendants and neck-rings, the silver coins, the pieces of amber and jet, the chessmen cut from ivory. None of it meant anything anymore.

'Good riddance to a pile of shit!' Nug said, squatting down and going back inside one final time.

Alan walked back to the pillaged relic-trays. They were now scattered over the grass, empty. Pins, tools, tabs, all lay useless. Pages of notepad scrawled with vital information fluttered about in the wind. A pang of regret went through him, but then he glanced up and saw the blood-stained megalith, with David's eviscerated body still lying at its feet, and his resolve hardened. He cast around on the floor for any tidbits of bone or metalwork that might have eluded them.

And that was when he heard the step behind him.

He glanced round, expecting to see Nug. Instead, he saw Linda ... and Ivar's femur, long, hard and curved like a bow as it swept round towards his face.

There was a crashing blow, a flash of light, then Alan was on the grass, his vision flickering and fading. The last thing he remembered seeing was Nug crawling head-first out from the barrow, and Linda standing to one side of him, entirely alone but, despite all the laws of physics, lifting the portal-stone high into the air.

ᚠᚢᚱᛏᚢᚾᚨ

When Alan came to, the wind was howling around him. Above, the sky was almost black, which in its turn reflected in a dark and truly terrible sea. Thunder reverberated through the heavens. In the far distance, lightning flickered. He glanced around closer to home, and was both chilled and revolted to find himself naked and bound upright against the megalith. His fetters were the entrails of David Thorson. They were cold and slick against his skin.

'Welcome back,' said a voice.

Alan glanced up. Linda stood directly before him ... or rather, what had once been Linda stood before him. She too was entirely nude, but now smeared all over with blood and brains, every inch of her sumptuous flesh coated in the viscous matter. It gleamed on her jutting breasts, matted the soft down between her thighs, was thoroughly worked into the now glutinous, tangled, spiked-up mane on her head. Only her eyes were unsullied; they shone like pale jewels in the midst of the frenzied, red and grey daubing.

'Oh ... oh, Jesus Christ,' Alan stammered.

She smiled a lupine smile; her canines seemed unnaturally pronounced between her ordure-caked lips. 'How often you Christians call on that God of yours.' She indicated the corpses of David and Nug – the latter with his head now a crushed, masticated pulp – lying side by side next to the barrow. 'And how often he fails to answer.'

'Linda,' Alan began, his voice breaking with terror, 'you've got to try and get a grip.'

Still she smiled. 'Ah yes, Linda. This is the body you desire, is it not?' She hefted her young breasts, squeezing the nipples between her thumbs and forefingers so that they expanded into ripe cherries. 'I've watched you from close. I've seen your hopeless yearning for it. Your desperate misery because it wasn't given over freely to you.'

Alan could only stare aghast at the horrible thing now taunting him. It looked like Linda, it spoke like Linda, it *was* Linda ... yet it wasn't. There was a frightening maleness about her cruel expression, about the way she held herself, about the threatening, brutish stance, the hunched neck, the glaring, hate-filled eyes.

'You should simply have taken it,' she advised. 'Whenever you wanted, with force. That would have been the warrior's way ... and so rewarding.' She rolled a thick, red tongue across her white teeth. 'Ah, the joy of spending in an unwilling cunt ... and spending hard, and then beating and disposing of that cunt, as it deserves, as we did the sacred virgins at Coldingham Abbey ...'

Alan didn't need to be reminded about that ghastly atrocity. In 870, Ivar attacked the nunnery at Coldingham on the Northumbrian coast. Among heathen nations, there'd been a great and lucrative slave-trade in holy women. On this occasion, the sisters had known about the coming raid in advance, and in a madness of terror, had taken blades and disfigured themselves, hoping to render themselves worthless as merchandise. It backfired. When he discovered what they'd done, Ivar's wrath was appalling to behold ...

'They thought to revolt us,' Linda scoffed. 'They did. But determined that it was our day, we took them anyway, again and again, in every way possible, in every hole, 'til they were worn out from us. And then, because we couldn't sell them, we burned them – *burned them!* – as punishment for the horrors they put us through.'

Alan tried not to visualise the awful spectacle of 200 inverted crosses along the shore, on each one a nailed naked body writhing as the flames licked at it from the heaped faggots beneath. He kicked and twisted in his slippery bonds, but for the moment at least they held him fast. 'Even your own people hated you,' he hissed.

'What matter?' Linda replied, 'so long as they feared me too.'

'You are pure evil.'

'No.' She shook her gory head. 'Evil is to neglect the gods. And as you can see,' she turned towards the sea, mountainous clouds racing over it on the storm wind, forks of lightning jabbing down, 'that is not the case where *I* am concerned. Is this not their approval, their gratitude that centuries on, their glory is re-awakened?'

'This is empty noise and fury!' Alan shouted. 'As your entire worthless, monstrous life was.'

She smiled again ... those teeth, that red steaming tongue. 'My monstrous life was only the beginning. As you shall see. Your wise-woman read my epitaph, did she not? Carved there on that stone behind you by my own brother, Halfdan. 'Great Ivar,' it says, 'Great Ivar sleeps here, closed up until the time is right for

Ragnarok. Woe unto him who awakens Ivar's wolf-kin, and frees that beast to roam in the world before the first day of the Fimbulvetr. For he shall reap a maelstrom of blood and fire!' '

For a moment, Alan couldn't answer. He knew that Professor Mercy had read and understood precisely that. It had been nonsense to think she hadn't been able to; there wasn't a Viking inscription in the world that Jo Mercy couldn't translate. She'd understood it all right, and it had terrified her; so much so that she hadn't dared repeat it. It all made sense now, of course, as did the reference to Ragnarok, and to the onset of the Fimbulwinter, the legendary winter at the end of the world.

'It's your fate to be destroyed with the other Norse demons, is it?' said Alan. 'That doesn't surprise me.'

Linda's eyes narrowed, but her grin remained; in fact, it broadened, grew even toothier, more vampiric. 'Nothing is fixed, Christian. Your simple folk lived in awe of the Final Day, when your White-Christ would come riding through the sky on a ball of flame. How could they have foreseen their own final day, when I, Ivar Ragnarsson, would come instead ... and eat them! Those Irish, those Saxons ... *I ate them*. In the great name of the Allfather.'

Alan shook his head, not wanting to acknowledge this: formerly the rumour, now the undeniable truth, that Ivar and his fellow berserkers would often devour the hearts and livers of those they slaughtered.

'And now,' she said slowly, almost tenderly, 'I eat you.'

Alan gazed up at her, saturated with sweat.

'The first of many,' she added, leaning towards him, drawing something from behind her. 'Before we cut the eagle on tearful Edmund's back, we submitted him to the arrow-fest, to see just how great an ordeal a Christian king could endure.'

Alan remembered the arrow ordeal too. Before they split King Edmund open, they hung him from a branch and shot him full of arrows, taking care all the while to penetrate no vital organ, to leave him bristling like a porcupine but still very much alive.

'Alas,' Linda said, 'in these uncivil times, we have no arrows. We do, however, have *this*.' She held out Clive's awl: the long steel pin with the handle of leather. And, without another word, she placed it against Alan's shoulder and thrust it deeply in.

He bit down on his tongue in his efforts not to scream. Blood flowed over his lips, but the agony of that was nothing compared to the agony in his shoulder, where the metal sank in like the clumsiest, most heavy-handed hospital injection, yet even then went on and on, running through muscle and sinew, and finally, with a dull *crunch*, pinioning the bone.

It wasn't courage alone that prevented Alan from shrieking. Initially he almost passed out, and hung there in a swoon. When she yanked the blade out again, he came violently round, however, and gave a helpless, chicken-like squawk.

'Weak,' she said. 'So weak.'

And she plunged the awl into him again, driving it this time to its very hilt in the thick, meaty part of his right thigh. Now he did scream. It was unavoidable, though half way through he tried to strangle it, and almost choked with the effort.

After the thigh, she went for the right biceps, thrusting the spike clean through it, so the point came out on the other side. Pride forgotten, Alan roared out, struggling frantically with the greasy ravels of gizzard, his entire body now running with blood.

After this, she stuck him in the side of the neck; he gagged as he felt the steel penetrate his trachea; the sensation of air starting to whistle in his violated throat was as much a source of horror to him as pain. Next, it was the turn of both his feet. The awl stabbed violently down, fully transfixing either instep. Then it was his left cheek, the tool forced in through his frothing mouth, then pushed out via the side of his face, gashing teeth and gums on the way. Alan cried and wept, and fought against his bonds, which were now stretching, though not quite enough for him to wriggle free of them.

Linda considered carefully where the next intrusion might be made. Then she took hold of his penis, held it upright and spread the urethra with her fingers. With her other hand, she placed the tip of the awl against it. She eyed his anguished face, amused. 'What do you think? A quick downwards thrust, or slow, steady infiltration?'

He shook his head, pleading. 'No ... no ...'

'It won't kill you,' she said. 'But the internal damage will be devastating.'

'Please,' he whispered.

'Courtesy of your final friend, I gave the Allfather new tribute.' She grinned contemptuously. 'The brain of Man. Which means the offering is almost complete. Yet there is one thing more. One further, final thing. And you know it.' She bared her teeth savagely. '*His manhood!*'

She drew her arm back to drive the awl down ... and a heavy piece of bone struck her across the shoulder and neck, shattering with the impact. It was the length of femur that Linda herself had used to knock Alan out. This time it was less successful. The possessed girl stumbled forwards, but was stung rather than injured. She whipped around with an enraged snarl.

Professor Mercy, unkempt beyond belief and visibly weakened by her own wounds, had crawled out from the entrance to the barrow and now stood there swaying, a fragment of leg-bone in one hand, the corroded mass of Ivar's broadsword in the other.

Linda gave a slow, scornful smile. 'You think to challenge me with those broken toys?'

The Professor nodded wearily. By the whiteness of her cheek, she was ready to faint, but she pressed on regardless: 'I think … I think to challenge you the way we English always challenged you Danes. In open combat.'

Linda's snarl curved into a grimace of glee. She at once struck a menacing martial arts pose, the awl still in her right hand, now clasped like a knife. 'It will be the greatest pleasure,' she said.

'And the greatest folly,' Alan growled, falling upon the girl from behind, looping the length of gut he'd finally slipped out of, around her neck, and pulling it tight as he dragged her down to her knees, then over onto her back.

Linda was taken completely by surprise. She thrashed madly, hissing, spitting, driving her elbows backwards, stabbing the awl over her shoulder at the face and throat of the man now struggling beneath her.

'Jo!' Alan gasped. 'Hit her … the sword …'

Professor Mercy came forwards uncertainly. Still fuddled, it took her several moments to comprehend what he was saying. She then threw down the piece of bone and raised the rusty sword over her head with both hands. Linda, meanwhile, had wriggled free of the intestine loop. She turned herself over and began to slam blow after blow into Alan's tortured, blood-soaked body. The awl punctured his ribs several times more, before the ancient sword came sweeping down and landed on the girl's skull with *thunking* impact.

The finely honed edge that had once hewn Christian limbs like matchsticks, had now dulled to a lumpy bluntness, and in fact it cut Linda only where pieces of it broke away. It was still a phenomenal blow. The girl fell heavily sideways, though she wasn't fully unconscious. Her hands clawed and clutched at the turf as though trying to draw strength from the Earth. For all that, the stroke had left a small furrow in the mussed, sticky mop of her hair, which was now filling up with blood of its own.

Professor Mercy lifted the sword above her head a second time. It was now bent at an alarming angle, and loose in its rotted hilt, but it was heavy and jagged, and still might kill if driven down hard enough. This time, though, she lacked the strength. Enfeebled by everything that had happened to her, she tottered sideways and dropped the blade to the grass.

Seizing her chance, Linda tried to crawl drunkenly away, but Alan scrambled in pursuit and began twisting coils of entrails around her. First he wound them around her torso, then he drew her arms behind her back and knotted her wrists together.

The Professor shook her head. 'She'll escape from that. *You* did.'

'By then we'll be gone,' Alan said, now binding the girl's legs. 'McEndry must be here soon; any time now.'

The Professor sank down onto her knees as she watched. Linda, though vaguely aware of what was happening, still lacked the power to resist effectively. Despite this, she was moving about ever more vigorously, attempting to look up, mouthing guttural curses. Alan continued to bind her as securely as he could, but all the while the wind was rising to hurricane velocity. The thundering of the waves below the cliff was now incredible. With such forces unleashed, it seemed unlikely anything could survive in the open for long, but still it got worse ... for then the lightning reached them, and began to strike with dread proximity. The first bolt hit the megalith. A searing zigzag of energy, it fleetingly split reality apart in a sizzling, fiery glare. The megalith burst asunder as though dynamited, splinters of stone flying in all directions. The heavens then erupted, and the rain began to fall in relentless, icy sheets.

'Enough, Alan,' the Professor cried, dragging at his arm. 'We have to get away from here ...'

He nodded, climbing painfully to his feet. Lightning flashed again, scorching the slope beside them, briefly igniting the grass, though the thrashing rain immediately doused it.

'Hurry,' the Professor shouted. 'She's the strongest among us, she's the one he wants. But if you've bound her too well, she'll be of no use to him ... *he'll come after one of us!*'

Despite the mayhem engulfing them, that terrible thought made sense, and Alan allowed the Professor to steer him from the now writhing, bucking form of the girl, down the suddenly treacherous slope and into the flimsy cover of the trees.

Even down there, the rain found them, bucketing through the evergreen canopy with astonishing force. They struggled on regardless, both still naked. Much of the blood had washed from Alan's white, rain-drenched body, but he leaned in agony against the woman, limping on feet that hurt like hot coals. All over the island, burning spears of electricity were crackling down, detonating among the tree-tops, glaring wetly on the high rocky massifs. The colossal booms of thunder set the very earth rocking.

'I can't see McEndry will even have set out in this,' Alan cried, as they stumbled past the blown-down remnants of their tents and along the side of the bog-pools, their waters overflowing as gallons of rain fell into them.

'It's come up from nowhere,' the woman replied. 'I've seen these Hebridean storms before. With luck, he'll already have set off. Let's just hope he made it.'

Once they broke out of the cover of the trees onto the open glen, the rain came down in a deluge so fierce it was nearly impossible to make headway against it. Cape Wrath was indeed aptly named. Yet amid all this noise and chaos, the real terror was still Ivar. As the fugitives ploughed along, finally moving uphill away from the marsh but plunging to their shins in brackish, peaty quagmires, Alan glanced continually back, expecting at any moment to see Linda's naked form, still painted in barbarous hues, come lithely out of the woods in pursuit. That thought alone drove him on. Even as the gradient steepened, and the rocks and stones cut into his feet, and the breath was like a knife in his wheezing lungs, he pushed himself as hard as he could. His pin-cushioned body was ravaged with pain, but escape was now all that mattered. And for the first time in as long as he could remember, escape suddenly seemed a possibility, for the head of the Stair was at last before them.

The swampy ground hardened and levelled out, and then they were tramping over flat rocks, and found themselves on top of the island's eastern bluffs. Directly in front of them, the ground fell away into a precipitous gully, at the base of which, explosions of foam revealed the point where rocks met sea, the noise of it vastly amplified up the great limestone chimney, the gale howling in their faces as though coming through a wind-tunnel. Still leaning against each other, they began to clamber down, buffeted, drenched, feet slipping and skidding among boulders not only loosely packed but now awash with rainwater.

'I can't ... I can't see McEndry!' Alan shouted.

'Keep going,' the Professor urged. 'He *must* be here.'

And, by the grace of God, he was.

The doughty Scot had been there for some time and, once the storm had blown up, had dragged his boat as far onto the shingle as he'd been able to. The two survivors were half way down the Stair before they were able to spot him. When they did, they began wildly shouting, coming down the remaining 80 feet of rubble at reckless speed. Several times they fell or caught themselves on juts of stone. McEndry, packed inside a heavy oilskin mac, and with a broad oilskin hat jammed down on his head, could only gaze up at them, astonished.

Neither Alan nor the Professor even paused to consider the bizarre sight they must have made; both nude, the boy visibly cut and bruised in dozens of places, the woman incredibly tousled, the pair of them wet through and bone-weary.

'What in the name of ... ?' the boatman began, as they descended onto the beach.

'We've got to go,' Alan jabbered. 'We've got to go

now – right now!'

McEndry shook his head. 'I can't put out on this sea. It's a miracle I even got here ...'

'Mr McEndry,' said the Professor firmly, 'do as he says. We have to go now!'

The boatman was still too stunned to make any real sense of this. He gazed up the Stair. 'Where are the rest?'

'You don't want to know,' the woman said, grabbing him by the lapels of the mac and turning him round to face her. 'Believe me, you don't want to know anything about what's waiting back there!'

'Or what might be on its way towards us right now,' Alan added.

Something about them – about the desperation in their haggard, harrowed faces; about the way they stood; the way they were dressed, or rather undressed; the way their eyes bulged like duck-eggs and their voices creaked with a hoarseness born only of incessant shrieking – made his mind up for him. John McEndry was a native of Cape Wrath. He knew its terrible moods and awesome powers; he also knew its weird history and its strange, hideous legends.

There was no real contest.

Without further ado, he turned and waved them towards the boat. The moment they were aboard, he began pushing it out into the surf, stopping only to help the two passengers as they hurled out the various boxes and food-parcels he'd shipped across the firth for them, but which now would only hamper their escape. Within two minutes they were all on board, all using oars and paddles to negotiate the narrow pathway back to open water. But only when the motor roared to life did they at last begin to gain real distance.

The vessel dipped and tilted alarmingly as it rode the ponderous swells. The rain drove into their faces, the wind screamed across the grey, rolling sea, ripping up swirls of spume. They ploughed on anyway, drenched repeatedly, rising and falling 'til they were sick to the pits of their stomachs, but even then the two passengers felt only relief that the crags of Craeghatir were falling behind them. And yet ... yet, there was something that drew their attention back.

Alan was the first to look. He was in the process of pulling on an old, bilge-stained sweater and a pair of oilskin trousers that the boatmen kept in a locker under his bench, when he felt the overwhelming urge to turn and stare. He did so, and the moment he did, he swore with such venom and volume that the others turned and stared as well. They were stunned to see a naked female figure standing atop the highest of the island's cliffs, spreading her arms and then throwing herself out into space in a perfect swan-dive.

'I don't believe it!' Alan screamed. *'That psychotic bitch!'*

Timeless moments seemed to pass as Linda's supple form plummeted the 200 feet to the ocean, gracefully but at shocking speed. When she hit the waves, she smashed straight through them with only the slightest spurt of foam.

'Jesus Christ Almighty!' McEndry bellowed, flinging himself against the tiller bar, bringing the outboard around.

'What the hell are you doing?' the Professor demanded, turning on him.

'Didn't you see?' he replied.

'I saw!' she said, still struggling to get into the spare mac he'd given her. 'Keep going! We have to get back to the mainland!'

'But she might've survived ...'

'She'll have survived all right,' Alan put in.

'I've got to go back and see,' McEndry insisted.

The outboard was now coming round in an arc that would take it directly back to the island. Frantically, the Professor tried to wrestle with the boatman. 'You'll kill us all,' she protested.

He shrugged her off, then bent down, opened another locker and drew out the orange packaging of a life-jacket. 'I don't know what ungodly things you people have been doing over there, but I'm not leaving anyone in this sea ...'

The professor looked at Alan hard. He immediately caught her meaning and, hefting the oar he'd been using, swung it round in a massive circle, slamming it against the back of McEndry's head. The Scot crumpled sideways in a senseless heap, and for a moment it was all Alan and the professor could do to save him from toppling overboard. However, by the time they'd dragged the unconscious man back over the gunwales, and laid him in the bilge, they were chugging back towards the island, and probably only 50 or 60 yards from its outer shoals.

Hurriedly, the Professor scrambled along the boat, to take charge of the tiller. Alan, meanwhile, still armed with his oar, stood at the prow, scanning the heaving waves for any sign of Linda. Tufts of weed, torn up from the sea-floor, were visible, clouds of sand and shingle could be seen roiling beneath the surface, but there was no trace of human life. The shadow of the island now fell across them; the water seemed darker, it was starting to break on the rocks and reefs. Alan turned back to the Professor, who had managed to get hold of the tiller-bar, but who, fearful of capsizing them, was attempting to bring the vessel about slowly and with care.

'She must've drowned,' he shouted. 'I can't see even Ivar lasting in this ...'

And the Professor screamed and pointed.

And before Alan could react, he felt claw-like hands seize hold of his left leg.

He looked down in astonishment. Linda had arisen beside the boat like some demonic mermaid. Washed clean of blood and filth, but grinning insanely, she had reached over the gunwales and taken hold of him. Instead of using him to try to climb aboard, however, she was yanking at him, doing everything in her not inconsiderable power to drag him down to her. Fleetingly, Alan had a vision of what that would entail: a slow descent into the icy, echoing deeps, Linda kicking down behind him with unnatural vigour, forcing him further and further down, a greenish, ochre darkness slowly enfolding them, until only the gleaming whites of her feral, wolf-like teeth were visible.

Petrified, he began swinging the paddle down onto the top of her head. But such was her strength that she'd already almost overbalanced him. If it hadn't been for the slick surface of the oilskin trousers, she'd probably have been able to take a proper hold and then exert massive pulling power. As it was, Alan's position was precarious enough. The boat swayed horrifically, and with every blow he aimed at the girl, his centre of gravity changed for the worse. He shrieked for the Professor to help him but, bewilderingly, she stayed where she was, fighting with the tiller.

'Jo, for Christ's sake!' Alan yelled.

Linda had now got his foot over the gunwale, and was hauling it down into the water. Inevitably, Alan toppled backwards and landed on his butt. As he did, the girl drew her body up and braced her feet against the side of the craft to give herself greater leverage. Alan cast frantically about to grab hold of anything he could, and kicked at her with his free foot. The heel impacted on her nose, flattening it so that blood shot across her face like raspberry ripple. Even the notion that he had once loved this misshapen creature had fled in the face of his desperation to survive. She might have been only a vehicle for Ivar's crazed spirit, but she was a vehicle that simply had to be destroyed. Alan kicked at her again and again. His heel now smashed into one of her eyes, mangling it, but still it made no difference. She rent and tore at him ferociously.

Alan glanced again towards Jo. Bafflingly, she was still leaning hard on the tiller. And then, in an instant, he realised what she was doing ... leaning on the bar so hard that the boat wasn't so much turning, as pivoting round on its axis. At once, Alan knew what the plan was; it was perhaps the only plan, but it would be no use unless ... unless ...

With a wild shout, he stood up and threw himself overboard.

He arched over Linda's head, and hit the raging water perhaps half a yard behind her. After being drenched by the rain and swept by the gale, the sea seemed almost warm in comparison, but it was still a terrific shock suddenly to crash down into that dark swell, salt bubbles swirling around him like angry wasps. Urgently, he fought his way back to the surface. He couldn't allow her to take him down. For her part, Linda – though not looking anything like Linda, looking more like the revenant of some torn, disfigured pirate – broke away from the boat and spun around to face him. Alan struck at her with his fist – futilely, for she caught him by the wrist. He struck at her with his other fist, and she caught that one too. And then she grinned. And it was the most monstrous, malicious thing he'd ever seen. He imagined her lunging forward and biting into his face, chewing on his nose and lips, on his throat even ...

But she'd never have the chance.

For in that last second, Alan ducked and swam away from her, diving down into the chill, rolling depths. Linda might have followed him had she not suddenly been distracted by the thunderous noise in her ears and the choking stench of fuel. She turned ... just as Jo Mercy rode the bows of the boat round towards her; the bows and the churning, chopping mass of steel that was the 125-horsepower propeller.

There was no time to escape.

Linda went under it with shrill, bubble-filled shrieks.

For several nightmarish seconds she writhed down there, white flesh, flailing hands, deep billows of swirling scarlet, all contrasting sharply with the sandy-grey of the sea.

From where he was, perhaps six feet down, Alan heard an agonised grinding and clanking of metal. Glancing back up, he saw only vague outlines, but he could easily detect thrashing flurries of movement, twisting tortured limbs ... then the oblong outline of the boat moving steadily away against the stark brightness of the sea-surface, and an object descending stiffly, wreathed in a murky mist of its own making. As it fell slowly past him, trailing clouds of fish-bait, he caught fleeting glimpses of an arm shorn off at the elbow, of an eviscerated upper torso, and of a skull clad only in threads of skin and hair, itself split five or six times over ... Then his air was ready to give out.

Alan kicked his way back to the surface and broke through the bloody waves, coughing and spluttering. Professor Mercy brought the boat back around, though it was much harder to navigate now with the propeller blades broken and dented. Only by throwing out the corded life-jacket did she manage to haul him aboard.

ᚠᚨᛚᛚᛖᚾ

Almost nothing was said. Their breathing was hoarse, heavy. In strained, soaked silence, they steered back towards the distant shadow of the mainland. Both of them noticed, though neither remarked on, the almost unnatural way the winds now seemed to drop and the oceans to calm. Soon the waters were chopping rather than swelling, the rain slowly petering out, spitting rather than thrashing. Still they said nothing. If it was a miracle, it had come six lives too late.

An hour later and half way back, McEndry began to stir. For a short time he didn't know where he was. He lay with his head cradled in Alan's lap as the craggy Scottish headlands emerged through the clearing banks of mist. The sun now broke out overhead, a dull red jewel swathed in cotton-wool. Shafts of light beamed down, and where they hit the rain-sodden land, there was a dazzling reflection. For a brief, illusory moment, it was all along the shoreline, as though the whole of Britain was in flames.

By pure chance, Alan glanced down at that moment, and saw those flames dancing in McEndry's dull, ox-like eyes. It wasn't reassuring to see a faint smile touch the seaman's crinkled old mouth.

THE HELLION

Rula was texting again as she trailed along at the back. By Keith and Sally's estimation, it was the fifth time she'd done it openly that weekend, and it was only mid-afternoon on the Saturday. Whether she thought Geoff just wouldn't notice or perhaps no longer cared was anyone's guess. But she was smiling to herself mischievously, like a schoolgirl, as she keyed in some quick, no doubt titillating message. Briefly, she was so absorbed that she didn't even hear as Sally called back to her across thirty yards of soggy moorland.

'Rula, you alright? Rula ...!'

'What? Oh yeah, everything's fine.' Rula pocketed the phone and trudged on. By her glazed eyes she was a long way from Lower Cringle Moor, North Yorkshire.

'What about this Raven Man?' Geoff asked Keith. He too had glanced back and seen the cause of the delay. But for the moment at least, he seemed indifferent to it.

'The "foul creature of Odin",' Keith said with forced enthusiasm. 'At least that was how it was described in the *Anglo-Saxon Chronicle*.'

'Foul creature of Odin, eh?'

'It was a kind of bird-man. Or so the legend tells us. Supposedly, it was invoked by Viking forces during their retreat from the Saxon king, Athelstan, after he smashed them at York in 927 AD, the idea being to conceal what little booty they hadn't already lost and put this thing on guard over it.'

'And did it work?' Geoff strode heavily, oblivious to the sporadic gusts of icy rain sweeping over them. He gazed directly ahead, mouth set in a firm line. By the looks of him, he couldn't actually have given two hoots whether invocation of the Raven Man had worked or not.

'Maybe the proof is in the fact this so-called treasure's never been found,' Keith replied, recollecting what he could of the little-known myth he'd uncovered during his recent researches. 'They supposedly buried it somewhere near an old temple to Thor, which by then was derelict.'

'*Thurmond* Priory,' Geoff said. '*Thor's Mound* maybe? Something like that, eh?'

'Not far off,' Keith replied. 'In old Norse, "Thurmond" means "Protected by Thor". Anyway, that's what the Normans thought ...' He zipped his padded anorak to just under his chin. The February wind wasn't simply wet, it was bitterly cold. 'During the Harrying of the North in 1069, they targeted Thurmond specifically. They searched for any sign of the Viking trove, but came away empty-handed. History doesn't record whether or they were driven off by a monstrous bird-man, though Hugh de Breteuil, who was the Norman baron involved, was beheaded by Hereward the Wake less than a year later.'

'And are we the first to go looking since?' Geoff wondered.

'Not as such. Thurmond Priory was built there in 1219. I'm sure the monks would have searched as well, but Thurmond was never notable for being a wealthy house, so I'm guessing they didn't find anything either. In 1540, it was closed down by Henry VIII's mob as part of the Dissolution of the Monasteries. It's on record that they looked too but got nowhere.'

'And what will *we* find when we get there?' Geoff said.

The directness of the question surprised Keith – as though it actually mattered to Geoff, despite his blank expression.

'What we'll find, Geoff,' Keith said, 'in all honesty, is a derelict Victorian house, which no-one wants anymore.'

'Well ... that would be about right. Something no-one wants anymore.'

On all sides of them, bleak moorland undulated away to indefinite, rain-smudged horizons. The sky was grey as asphalt; the tussocky grass had that broken, barren look you always saw in the wake of January snow. Ostensibly, they were following a well-trodden path, though in truth it was likely to be minimally trodden at this time of year. The North York Moors were a hugely popular environment for walkers, pony-trekkers, campers, picnickers, but not so much in February. The mood was worsened of course by the current status of Geoff and Rula. They'd been good friends to Keith and Sally for over a decade now, but not for much longer, Keith suspected.

A fast-flowing beck appeared in front of them. On Keith's OS map it was nothing: a meandering pale-blue line, thin as an eyelash. The real thing probably matched that image perfectly on a dry summer's day, but now it had swollen dramatically, not just with the recent rain, but with meltwater from the heavy snow of the previous month, transforming itself into a thundering, foaming torrent at least twenty yards across, maybe more. A narrow, timber footbridge led over it. The normal distance between the underside of the bridge and the beck's surface would be about three or four feet, but at present was less than a couple of inches. In fact, water continually swamped the structure, frothing over the top of it, causing it to visibly judder.

Keith halted, chewing his lip. 'Sorry guys, this could be a bit of a problem.'

He expected sympathy, perhaps under usual circumstances even a snigger or two. The rest of the crew were pretty used to his esoteric interests. They rarely took a weekend away together or even a daytrip to the country without him trying to fit in a quick visit to some famously mysterious place so that he could photograph it and later feature it on his blog, *Arcana UK*. It never took long. Mostly it was no more than a brief diversion from what would likely be a pleasant day spent taking in some awesome scenery and enjoying a nice pub lunch. But the weather had deteriorated since they'd left the car in a layby about a mile behind them, this issue with Geoff and Rula had soured the atmosphere, and now it seemed they couldn't go any farther anyway. It was difficult to imagine that anyone would find this funny. Geoff certainly didn't, but neither did he stop. Instead, he made a bee-line for the bridge. Though a natural-born outdoorsman and the fittest among them, he would ordinarily step back if they reached some kind of obstacle and be sure to assist the two ladies first. This time he strode ahead, clumping heavily across, slipping only once on the drenched woodwork, but keeping himself upright with the handrails, until he'd reached the other side, where he stopped and turned.

The rash act seemed to bring Rula out of her reverie. 'Geoff!' she said, yanking back her hood. 'What're you playing at?'

Geoff ignored her, addressing Keith and Sally. 'See ...' He tapped the bridge with his boot. 'Solid as a rock.'

Despite this, it still quivered with the force of river crashing past underneath. It wasn't exactly a rotten structure. But it didn't look new. They hesitated.

'Come on!' Geoff urged them. 'We're not going all the way back now, are we? Keith, do you want to see this Thurmond place or not?'

Keith glanced at Sally, who regarded the bridge nervously, before stepping forward and staring down at the roaring, swirling waters.

'We've come an awful long way just to give up!' Geoff called.

Shaking her head and hitching her rucksack, Sally shuffled out onto the bridge, gloved hands firmly grasping the rails to either side. 'It's shaking a bit, but it feels alright,' she said, venturing forward. 'One at a time though. It's taking a right battering.'

The others watched with baited breath, but in the end she made it without too much trouble. Keith turned to Rula. 'After you, love.'

Her gaze flickered towards him. 'Does this river look like it's rising to you, Keith?'

Keith contemplated that. It wasn't a pleasant thought – that getting to the other side now might not be as much of a problem as coming back the other way later on. The sky was no longer grey, it was purple. It wasn't just the worsening weather – time was getting on and dusk approaching, but ever fiercer squalls of icy rain blasted over them.

'We're pretty close to the place now,' he finally said. 'We'll be back here in no time.'

Immediately, he felt bad for telling her such a lie, especially as it was so self-serving. The truth was they were at least another half-mile from Thurmond Priory, while the only shelter anywhere near was a dilapidated shed, a byre or something, set a dozen or so yards back from the other shore of the beck, though that too was swaying in the gale; half its roof had already caved in. Despite that, Keith would sooner they were out here in the teeth of the elements than cooped up in the car again, ears reverberating to that lingering, wordless hostility between Geoff and Rula, which they'd endured all the way here from The Wayland, not to mention at the hotel dinner table the evening before. It was increasingly difficult for Keith and Sally to maintain the pretense that this excruciating turn of events wasn't ruining their tenth anniversary weekend. They'd agreed the night before, once ensconced back in their bedroom, that they'd try not to let it, but Keith had known it wasn't going to last. He didn't feel entirely sympathetic towards Rula anyway. Okay, Geoff might not have been the man for her, but it was a pity she couldn't have discovered that sooner in their marriage, preferably before she'd started playing around with someone else, albeit virtually.

So he too went across the bridge.

Once out in the middle, the rumble of the beck was deafening. He felt the vibrations in his legs; wavelets sloshed over the tops of his hiking boots. But he reached the other side, and when he glanced back, Rula was crossing as well. She was only half way over before Geoff turned and set off again along the moorland path, bypassing the shed without a glance. Sally shot Keith one of those quick, desperate looks that had become all too familiar since the weekend had commenced, and indicated they should wait.

Rula grimaced with discomfort as Sally helped her back onto firm ground again – by the looks of it, her boots were also squelching with water. 'Better be worth it, this place,' she grumbled.

'Believe it or not, this *whole* area's quite interesting,' Sally said, loyally regurgitating the stuff Keith had fed to her during the two-hour drive from Manchester the previous afternoon. 'Aren't there some relics of villages that got wiped out by the plague somewhere around here as well, Keith?'

'Not the plague,' he replied sharply, feeling annoyed that Rula was suddenly annoyed. 'It was smallpox. Mid-sixteenth century ...'

'There you go,' Sally said coolly. 'Smallpox. Told you this place was great.'

Keith Blackrock was a property surveyor by trade. His wife Sally was a dental nurse. They were both in their early thirties. Sally was a petite blonde, slim and girlishly pretty. Keith, on the other hand, was Mr Average: average height and build, thinning on top and with plain looks. They had one daughter, Tina, who was six years old, and currently staying with Sally's mother. Despite the appalling weather forecast, everything had looked set for a fun weekend, especially because as usual, their friends Geoff and Rula Wade were coming with them.

Geoff and Rula weren't too far off their own tenth wedding anniversary either, but it was now evident they weren't going to make it to the happy day. Not together.

From an outside perspective, it was difficult to pinpoint where it had begun to go wrong between them. Geoff, who was tall and rangy – something of a beanpole in fact, but at the same time handsome and energetic – was partly responsible. As Sally had observed over many years, he wasn't the most affectionate of husbands.

It wasn't unusual for him to leave Rula alone at parties and spend all night drinking and laughing with the men, or to send her off to the other end of the country on her own if she ever wanted to visit her parents in Bournemouth. Whenever he made trips himself, usually overseas in his capacity as software salesman, he'd never suggest taking her with him, and made no effort to contact her while he was over there, even if he was away several days or more. But Rula had damaged the relationship too, perhaps more so than Geoff. Having suffered the misfortune of a miscarriage very early in their marriage, which had left her unable to have children, it now seemed that she was permanently 'off sex', or so Geoff had once drunkenly confided in Keith. And given how attractive Rula was – a shapely redhead with sensual feline looks and a saucy sense of humour – that must have been doubly painful for him. Though he'd tried various methods by which to win her affections – everything from candle-lit romance to costumed role-play – Rula had remained unresponsive, eventually taking to sleeping in a separate bed and different room, because she found his 'mauling about in the middle of the night' irksome.

To their wider circle of friends, everything had appeared to be fine, but Sally and Keith were close enough to Geoff and Rula to know that it wasn't, and had watched in growing alarm as all these factors had slowly prised the once loving twosome apart. However, the death-blow had only fallen recently, when some creep at the local authority office where Rula worked had begun soliciting her favours. Sensing her growing disenchantment at home, as these creeps so often seem able to, he'd casually started paying her the attention she was missing from her husband, exchanging banter with her, sharing jokes and happy stories, making a cup of tea for her when she hadn't asked for one, always commiserating with her. Regardless that the creep was already married and had two children of his own, Rula had assured a stunned Sally that this was all 'completely above board'. He was just being a friend when she needed one. Except that now, only a few months later, that friendship had apparently extended to sexy texting. And to make matters worse, Geoff had somehow found out about it.

Of course, the tenth anniversary holiday had been booked well before all this had come out: a long weekend at Keith and Sally's favourite country inn, The Wayland Arms on the North York Moors.

'So what do we do?' Keith had said. 'Cancel it? Just because Rula's so self-centred that she thinks she's being swept off her feet by some office Lothario, when in reality he's a scrote whose sole interest is getting his leg over?'

'It's not that,' Sally had said reproachfully. 'I think she's genuinely fallen out of love with Geoff.'

'Either way, it doesn't help us much.'

'Now who's being selfish?'

'So that's the place, is it?' Geoff's voice cut through Keith's thoughts.

They'd crested a low ridge and had started down the other side into a shallow vale, in the very centre of which a house was visible, the first man-made structure they'd seen since the shed by the beck. Even from a distance of several hundred yards, it wasn't the grand edifice Keith had been expecting. This was no country mansion with sizeable outbuildings and parkland. True, its immediate perimeter was fenced and there looked to be a stable block of some description, but the main building was roughly the size and shape of a slightly larger-than-average suburban townhouse. That said, all the symbols of antique Victoriana were there: steep gables, towering chimneys and a central pyramidal tower, from the topmost spire of which some kind of dark flag or ragged mass of black, shapeless cloth billowed in the breeze. But it was also clear that the place was dilapidated: gutters hanging down, joists exposed through broken roof tiles, planks covering empty casements. On one hand Keith was glad of this, as it meant he'd get some genuinely spooky photos, but on the other it hardly enhanced the mood. The rain was now falling with greater intensity, the wind lashing it into them like bullets – all of which had drained not just their enthusiasm, but their energy. The moorland walk had fast become a chore rather than a pleasure, and in truth this didn't seem like much of a reward at the end of it.

'The Raven Man's supposed to tear people to pieces, is he?' Geoff asked, apparently oblivious to all this. 'When they visit the Priory, I mean?'

'Sorry?' For a second Keith thought he'd misheard. 'Where've you got that from?'

'The internet.' Geoff didn't look round as he plodded on. 'You already told us we were coming here, so I looked it up on my iPad last night.'

'Oh ... right.' This was the first time Geoff had ever shown anything more than polite interest in Keith's hobby.

'I mean, how else is it supposed to guard the treasure?' Geoff asked.

'It's only a fairy tale. I think you'll find it defies logical analysis.'

They reached the property's drive – a hard, stony track, which, while they'd approached the building from the southeast, meandered across the moor from the northwest. It bore no tyre-marks, implying no-one had been here since last summer at the latest, when the ground had been firmer, but if nothing else it would make easier walking from this point on. Keith glanced around. The women were approaching side-by-side, exchanging words whenever the rain and wind permitted. For the moment at least, possibly because the wild conditions and rugged landscape were interfering with the signal, Rula wasn't bothering with her mobile.

Just ahead, the drive was partially blocked by a rusted gate chained shut between two tall brick posts. On the left one, the words THURMOND PRIORY had been engraved on a slate plaque, while on the other there was some kind of family crest depicting a huge birdlike object with immense spread wings and two battle-axes crossed over its breast. Keith fished his camera out and snapped a couple of pictures. In the rapidly fading light of late afternoon, he used a flash, which glittered on the rainwater trickling down over the eroded lettering. All very dramatic, he thought, though he took pains to ensure the gate itself wasn't exposed in the shot. At some time in the past, the original gate, which probably was pretty ornate, had been removed and replaced by what looked like a spare entry-gate to a farm field – this latter was fastened shut with a modern padlock, and wore a 'Keep Out' notice painted on a plank. It would be easy enough to climb over it, but it trashed any aura of the Gothic. The house meanwhile posed no such problem. It stood about fifty yards beyond the gate, a hulking, rain-drenched outline on the leaden sky. The flag or whatever it was Keith had seen cluttering the spire seemed to have blown away in the wind.

'I thought this place would be some kind of church,' Geoff said, gazing up at it.

'Like I say, the actual priory got dissolved by Henry VIII,' Keith replied. 'The prior and his chief monks got hanged, drawn and quartered for encouraging the Pilgrimage of Grace. Afterwards, the place stood empty until local people began raiding it for stone and timber. There were stories of officials visiting the area a few decades later and being disgusted at the sight of pillars and pedestals built into cottages and pig-sties, ornamented arches covering the entrances to cowsheds, all that stuff. The name would have lingered, though ... "Priory". Long enough for it to get used again when someone finally came along and decided to build a new house here.'

'But the Raven Man's still supposed to be lurking around?'

Keith glanced sidelong at him, curious as to his ongoing interest in this more grotesque aspect of the tale.

'If the treasure's still here, I suppose he must be,' Geoff said, answering his own question. 'Presumably he still thinks he's got a job to do, guarding it.'

'Geoff ...' Keith said. 'There's no such thing as the Raven Man. You realise that? It's just a myth, Dark Age nonsense. There's never been a single case of any person found killed in this vicinity, certainly not torn to bits. The Vikings will have spread the story to scare people off. That's all.'

'The gold's real then?'

'It's thought to be, but no-one's ever found it, and I doubt we'll be here long enough to look for it ourselves.'

The women now arrived, peering up at the house with no little apprehension, though Geoff was unconcerned by that. He quickly clambered over the gate, leaving the others no option but to follow. Beyond it, they tramped a final fifty yards of drive – again it was stony and compact rather than muddy, indicating that no passing vehicles had ploughed it up any time recently – and entered the forecourt to the main building. This comprised an old, overgrown lawn, the grass and thorns that straggled across it brown and withered, and a parking area of rutted grit crazy-paved with pools of water.

The frontage of Thurmond Priory lowered over them. Despite the severe toll the years without occupancy had taken on it, there was still plenty of evidence that it had been a handsome structure in its day, with neatly patterned brickwork and well-appointed windows. The family crest was again displayed above the top of the main entrance, though a corrugated iron sheet had been fastened over the door itself, and most of the ground-floor windows were barred with planks, though several of these had rotted and fallen away, revealing dank, skull-like sockets. Rainwater dripped from the eaves, while pieces of broken slate and pipework strewed the footings.

'Wonder why it's just been left like this?' Rula said.

'Probably part of an estate that hasn't gone through probate,' Keith replied. 'Absentee heirs, or something.'

'What ... they'd just leave it here, decaying?'

'Depends on the solicitors. They could be dealing with hundreds of other properties at the same time. Plus it's miles from anywhere. Where are they going to find a caretaker to come and spruce this place up?'

It was a humdrum explanation, but that didn't reduce the romance of it in Keith's eyes. Eagerly, he snapped a few more shots. Possibly as an antidote to the mundane nature of his job, in recent years he'd developed a deep fascination with the eerie and macabre. His blog was a celebration of all that was ghoulish, particularly if it had a British setting and British folklore associations, and especially if connected to places Sally and he could visit during their trips around the country. With the background story to Thurmond, and the dramatic conditions they'd found here, this couldn't have been better for his purpose; the only danger was that said conditions might spoil the quality of his pictures. But he was determined to give it a go.

'Haven't you finished yet?' Sally eventually asked. Five minutes had become ten, and then twenty, as Keith sought ever more spectacular angles from which to shoot the neglected pile of brick. 'Keith ... we could do with getting back.'

He glanced around. Even in their waterproofs, the two women were like drowned rats, huddled together shivering. This wouldn't be the first time during a weekend jaunt when they'd followed him to some semi-inaccessible spot which to those less versed in the weird would seem like a blot on the landscape, but there was a real sense of wildness and isolation in this place, especially with twilight falling. It was no surprise that he'd got carried away, but equally that they weren't keen to loiter here.

'Yeah, I'm done.' He inserted his camera into its leather case. 'We can split ...'

'Whoa!' Geoff interrupted. 'Don't you at least want to look inside?'

'What are we going to find inside, Geoff?' Rula wondered. 'It's just an empty house.'

He ignored her. 'We obviously can't go in through the front, but let's check around the back ... see if we can find a window or something?'

Keith glanced at Sally, who shrugged wearily, and said: 'Anything to get out of the rain, I suppose. But let's not take too long.'

They trooped around the exterior of the house, taking a narrow passage on its east side. More slates and fragments of birds' nests scattered the greasy flagstones. In a recess half way along, they encountered an open door which was partly concealed by hanging ivy. Geoff fought his way through first, and then stepped back so the rest could enter. Inside lay a warren of damp, dusty rooms, most indistinguishable from one another in terms of their bare floorboards and drab, peeling walls. The reek of mildew was so thick it was almost tangible. Deep dimness pervaded, only the occasional shaft of half-light penetrating around the edges of loose or lopsided planking. Outside, the moorland wind was a muffled drone.

Geoff activated the reading-light on his iPhone, but as they explored, the atmosphere in the place turned steadily more oppressive. The sense of abandonment was overwhelming, as if it was so long since anyone had lived here that time itself had forgotten who they were, and yet … it seemed like a cliché, but Keith for one didn't feel as if they were quite alone. The clumping of their footfalls echoed, the rain hammered on the wood and stone enclosing them.

'We're not the first to get curious about this place,' Geoff said.

They'd passed the bottom of the main stairway, and entered the largest of the downstairs reception rooms, where his light now picked out a stone fireplace, which wasn't just blackened by soot but had an extensive pile of torn-up floorboards propped alongside it.

'Some tramp probably,' Keith said, not encouraged by that thought, though from the strands of cobweb draped over the firewood, no-one had made a fire here recently.

'And look at this,' Geoff added.

He'd pivoted slowly around, and on the wall facing the fireplace found what looked like evidence of arson. More lengths of splintered wood had been propped against this wall and set alight. It hadn't done a great deal of damage, aside from charring what remained of the wallpaper and creating a great black smoke-stain which spread up and outward in either direction as though extending a colossal pair of wings.

Keith was mesmerised. He slipped his camera from its case and took several more shots, this time slowly and carefully, ensuring everything was just right.

'I don't blame someone for trying to burn this place down,' Sally said with a shudder.

'Whoever it was, they didn't get very far,' Geoff replied. 'Wonder why?'

'Place is probably damp to its foundations,' Keith said.

Geoff glanced at him, as though amused by the prosaic explanation.

'Perhaps we should build our own fire?' Rula said. 'If nothing else we can get warm.'

Sally glanced at Keith. 'Surely we're not going to be here that long?'

'I'm ready to go now,' he retorted.

'Nah, let's dry off a bit first,' Geoff said. He slumped to his knees in front of the hearth, and commenced restocking it with fresh kindling from the woodpile.

Sally looked shocked. 'Seriously?'

'It'll warm us up a bit as well.' If Geoff could sense her bewilderment, he didn't respond to it. Instead, he selected larger pieces of lumber and set those in place too. 'We've got a long walk back in the cold and rain. In the meantime, that man of yours can get some decent interiors for his blog.'

Keith was as bemused by this as Sally. Geoff was quite the alpha-male when the mood was on him, but he rarely assumed a leadership role during these trips to the country, knowing this was more Keith's territory. That said, he was right about the weather. The house shuddered to the strengthening wind; rainwater literally sluiced through the gaps between the boards.

'Can't do any harm to get dry, I suppose,' Keith said.

Sally glanced at Rula for support, but Rula was checking her mobile again, openly disappointed to find there was still no signal. Sally folded her arms with irritation, but said nothing else.

Geoff soon got the fire going. In retrospect, that was more of an achievement than Keith initially gave him credit for. They had matches as part of the safety kit they always took whenever traipsing outdoors, the wood was dry and the wind down the chimney did its bit to fan the flames, but there was no fire-starter and only a few bits of rag to act as touch-paper. The blaze rose nevertheless, filling the room with shimmering light and warmth. They gathered in front of it, palms outstretched.

'This wasn't a bad shout,' Keith said.

Geoff acknowledged the compliment with a dispassionate nod.

Then they heard the first *thud*.

The place was already alive with creaks and taps. But this was something else. A loud, reverberating thump. An impact perhaps, rendered even more noticeable by a series of follow-up thumps occurring at regular intervals of one every second or so.

One by one, they became aware of it.

'Is that upstairs?' Rula asked.

They glanced at each other uneasily. Geoff strode to

THE HELLION

the doorway, and gazed up the stair. He shook his head. 'No-one there ... but, I dunno, from here it sounds like it's round the back. I'll check.'

Keith made to go with him, but Sally grabbed his arm. 'Keith ... if there's someone else here, we should leave.'

Keith agreed with her, but Geoff – as increasingly seemed to be his reckless manner during this trip – had already lurched out of sight, his footsteps receding as he headed towards the back of the building. Keith hurried after him.

As soon as Keith stepped from the fire-lit room, the clammy chill re-embraced him. Dusk was now falling properly, so it was darker out there than before, though some twenty yards to his right he saw Geoff's rangy shape disappearing through another door. He hurried in pursuit, joining his friend in what might once, judging by its grimy brick floor and the jagged nozzles of pipework jutting from its rotted walls, have been a kitchen. There were several unboarded windows in here, but they were thick with greenish filth. This partly obscured the courtyard space beyond them, but not sufficiently to conceal the nearest corner of the stable block, where a lower section of door was banging in the wind.

'That explains that,' Keith said, relieved.

'Yeah, but why wasn't it doing that when we first arrived here?' Geoff wondered. 'Has someone just unlocked it or something?'

'Geoff ... what does it matter? I've got what we came for. We can go.'

Geoff glanced at him sceptically. 'You want to go back across that moor in this weather, Keith?'

'We came out in it.'

'It wasn't as bad then as it is now?'

That was true, but Keith was baffled that Geoff seemed to be suggesting they should stay here until the storm abated. Full darkness was no more than quarter of an hour away, and the rain-soaked path they'd used to get here had been difficult enough even in daylight. Geoff tested the kitchen door handle. It turned; the door opened. He stepped outside.

'Geoff ...?' Keith followed.

Again, the cold and the wet assailed him, taking his breath away. Meanwhile Geoff dashed towards the stable, head bowed. Keith accompanied him, sploshing through ankle-deep puddles. As they reached the stable door, it banged closed in front of them, jamming in its frame.

'There's your mystery,' Keith shouted. 'The wind catches it one way, slams it, catches it another way and it springs loose.'

Geoff leaned over the door, which came to about waist-height, and stared up into the unlit recesses of the stable roof. Keith gazed up too. Initially, he saw only blackness, but gradually the outlines of rafters and hanging chains emerged.

'What are we looking for?' he asked.

'Not sure,' Geoff replied. 'Thought I heard something.'

'Well, it's blowing a racket out here ...'

Geoff raised his hand for silence, which irritated Keith. Obediently, he listened again, but heard nothing that couldn't have been caused by the gale. Despite this, he leaned over the lower door and peered hard into the darkness above. Fleetingly, he imagined that part of it – a part that was somehow darker than all the rest – was moving; slowly and sluggish, as though crawling along the underside of the ceiling. He even fancied trickles of dust were descending, but they were just as likely the result of the wind hammering the flimsy structure. He blinked and the optical illusion had gone.

'I'm going back inside,' he said. 'This is getting daft.'

Geoff grunted some incoherent reply, and Keith loped back across the yard. The wind was now so cold that it cut like a sword, and set him staggering even in that restricted space. Heading across open moor in this, especially in darkness, would be extraordinarily dangerous. He re-entered the house, panting and dripping, and sidled down the passage to the main room, the warmth and firelight of which was slowly spreading through the ground floor. As he did, he overheard the women talking.

'We argued badly in the room last night,' Rula said. It slowed Keith to a halt by the foot of the staircase. 'Not long after we'd said goodnight to you two. It was awful. Some vicious things got said ... by both of us. Anyway, Geoff stormed out and slept in the car.'

'Slept in the car?' Sally replied, incredulous.

Keith shared his wife's astonishment. If nothing else, they'd hoped the relaxed atmosphere of a beautiful country inn like The Wayland would have had some kind of healing effect on Geoff and Rula. Futilely, by the sound of this.

'What ... you mean all night?' Sally asked.

'For about four hours,' Rula replied. 'When he came back in, he was frozen to the core. I had to warm him up.'

'Well ... at least you'd both have enjoyed that.'

'Not warm him up the way you mean. I gave him the bed while I took the armchair.'

'Oh, Rula ...'

'There's nothing there anymore, Sal.' Rula didn't even sound tearful as she admitted this. Glum yes, but also resigned to her fate – and to Geoff's presumably. 'I don't feel about him the way I used to. It would be cruel to pretend otherwise.'

Keith now heard Geoff lumbering up the passage behind him. He swung around and pointed up the stairs. 'How about we check the bedrooms out? Like you say, might as well give the *whole* place a going-over while we're here.'

If Geoff was puzzled by Keith's apparent change of heart, he didn't show it. Merely nodded. Keith glanced quickly into the living room as they passed. The women were seated on the floor in front of the fire. They'd removed their boots and socks, which were suspended from the mantel above the flames. Sally was in the process of digging into her rucksack, extricating a flask and a couple of packets of sandwiches.

'Keith?' Sally called out as she heard them ascending the stair.

'Yeah, it's just us. That banging was nothing. A loose door. We'll not be a sec.'

There was more light upstairs than down, as most of the upper windows were uncovered by boards, but it was no less dismal a scene: rotting lathes exposed through semi-collapsed ceilings; hanging strips of mouldering wallpaper.

And something else.

They first saw it near the top of the staircase, on the banister and newel post, and then on the walls and doors of the landing: multiple sets of claw-marks, in each case three aligned hooks, or perhaps curved fingernails, having rent the plaster and woodwork. Geoff activated his phone-light again, so they could assess the markings properly – it wasn't encouraging. In all instances, the triple-slashes were deep, but also without rhyme or reason; and they were everywhere, in a mindless pattern – as if the whole upper interior of the house had developed a rash.

'You *sure* your Raven Man's only a legend?' Geoff asked.

Keith shrugged, but took pictures nevertheless. 'This'll just be someone's idea of a joke.'

'If you say so …'

They moved on, finding all the doors up there ajar, save one in the middle of the landing, which when they tested it was locked. A large master-bedroom, a gutted shell now, occupied the back of the house, facing due south. Its panoramic window had previously been fitted with leaded panes, but had shattered long ago, only fragments of stained glass remaining around its edges. They hovered there, peering out. The wind was blowing from the northwest, but snatches of it occasionally gusted backward, throwing icy rain into their faces. The last vestige of daylight fizzled out on the western horizon, yet briefly the harsh landscape was visible as clots of broken cloud scurried past the moon, exposing a bleak wilderness strewn with boulders and glinting a glacial silver.

'You've seen she's actually been texting the bastard in my presence?' Geoff said, somewhat unexpectedly. 'What do you think about that, Keith? In all honesty.'

'I don't know,' Keith answered. And in truth, he didn't. Before all this, he'd loved Rula – both as a close friend in her own right, and as the lovely wife of an even closer friend. Yet, though he accepted that most marital breakdowns were the responsibility of both parties, it was difficult to maintain respect for her when he saw such casual infidelity as she'd displayed earlier. By the same token, of course, that also demonstrated how broken her and Geoff's relationship really was. Keith now felt they should *officially* break it, stop pussyfooting around and go their separate ways. At present, the whole thing was torturous – not just for Geoff and Rula, but for those forced to witness it.

'I don't even feel hostile to this guy at the office, whoever he is,' Geoff said. 'He's obviously a chancer, Rula's a looker ... you can't totally blame him.'

This was a higher philosophy Keith didn't entirely share, but he kept his mouth shut. He could offer no solution, no consolation. As if sensing this, Geoff looked to change the subject – a sudden bombardment of heavy hailstones gave him the opportunity.

'Wind, darkness ... now an ice-storm. Easy to imagine Vikings on a landscape like this.'

'They were well-beaten, the ones who came here,' Keith replied, glad to be discussing something else. 'I mean, they re-invaded later, but Athelstan was a hardcase. He kicked their arses again, and he *really* kicked them the second time.'

'Perhaps that's why they started using mythical monsters to do their dirty work?'

'Myth meant something in those days, that's for sure,' Keith agreed. 'To the Christians, the Raven Man was what they called a "hellion".'

Geoff looked intrigued. 'A what?'

'A hellion ... a demonic being charged with doing evil on Earth. Not as easy to disregard as other monsters.'

'No?'

'Well think about it ... God was real, the Devil was real. Therefore the Devil's creatures were real. Course, the Vikings didn't see the Raven Man as evil. In Norse myth, the raven had multiple purposes. Odin had two of them for pets, Hugin and Munin. They were battle-birds ... they'd peck the eyes out of his enemies, and feast on the corpses of the slain. But they were messengers too, and advisors. They had a positive role. The whole concept of the divine raven was commemorated for centuries by the Vikings on their black raven banner, which they called "Land-Waster".'

'Land-Waster ...' Geoff grinned crookedly as he surveyed the desolate terrain.

'Sounds terrifying, but it gave them courage in foreign countries, reminded them of home, their culture ...'

'While they were busy murdering and plundering, you mean?'

'Remember ... when they came here, they'd just been kicked out of York, which at the time was their city. Athelstan had attacked them ruthlessly. They were on the run.'

'Two sides to every tale, eh?' Geoff said.

'That's usually the way, isn't it?'

'One man's hellion, another man's angel.'

'Like I said ... ultimately there was no Raven Man. It would just be a warning the Vikings put out. It meant "don't touch our stuff!"'

Geoff looked disappointed. 'You're saying there was no rune-magic involved at all?'

Keith glanced quizzically at him. 'Rune-magic? Which website were you looking at last night?'

Geoff gave another brooding smile. 'It was a bit fanciful, I'll admit.'

'Sounds it.'

'*Monsters of Old Britain*. It said the Raven Man was invoked by rune-magic. And that his task wasn't just to protect the hidden gold but to destroy anyone who trespassed in this place.'

'People came and lived here. He can't have been very good at his job, can he?'

'But they don't live here anymore, do they, Keith.' Geoff's smile had faded; his hooded eyes seemed to fix on the tumult outside.

'The girls have got some nosh down there,' Keith said, deciding he'd had enough of this conversation too. 'You hungry?'

'Not really. *You* go.'

Keith hung around for a second, but then nodded, left the room and headed back downstairs, meeting Sally at the bottom. She'd pulled her socks, boots and anorak back on, but grabbed him before he could enter the main room.

'What're you doing up there?' she hissed.

'I wanted to give you two some space,' he said.

'You mean so I could learn something I don't already know? I think we've been here long enough, don't you?'

'Yeah but … Geoff's weirding me out. Now he won't come down.'

She looked puzzled. 'You mean he's sulking?'

'I think it's a bit more than that.'

'Well … we can't stay *here*.'

'That's another problem. The weather out there is beyond foul.'

Sally listened, finally seeming to notice the louder, more violent impacts as millions of gobbets of ice showered across the house. 'Christ, is that hail?'

'Yeah, but listen … soon as it clears, we'll go for it. Get Rula ready.'

'What about Geoff?'

'I'll go up and talk to him. See if I can get some sense

into him.'

Keith trotted back up the stairs, heading into the master-bedroom. Only to find that Geoff was no longer standing by the window – in fact that he wasn't even in the room.

'Geoff?' Keith shouted, ambling back out onto the landing. 'Yo, Geoff!'

There was no response. Keith moved from room to room, calling Geoff's name. But still there was no response. No response at all.

They split up and spent several minutes combing the house and its outbuildings, frantically calling Geoff's name, though outside at least their voices were lost in the storm. Keith halted again in front of the stable door. For some reason, the dank blackness within this time felt different – as if the stable was finally empty, as if whatever had been lurking in there before, waiting and listening, was no longer present. Keith knew this was pure fancy, his imagination running on overload thanks to the air of isolation in this woe-begotten spot, but even so he wished he'd had a torch with which to search the decrepit structure properly. His mobile was a more dated model than Geoff's. It boasted no reading-light facility, and as Rula had discovered, at present there wasn't even a signal by which to place a call.

He spent another two or three minutes trying to do just that, walking back and forth across the courtyard, repeatedly tapping in Geoff's number. Rather unexpectedly, on the eighth or ninth attempt, he made a connection. He progressed warily back to the house, holding the phone aloft. Still the call went through. As he re-entered the kitchen, he heard the *Garry Owen* march of the Seventh Cavalry somewhere on the floor above.

Sally and Rula met him at the foot of the staircase.

'That's Geoff's phone!' Rula said. The apparent genuine concern she'd shown since Geoff had gone missing was still a bit of a surprise to Keith.

'I know,' he replied, taking the stairs two at a time. 'I've just got through.'

Up on the landing it was so dark that initially he was disoriented. Occasional flickers of moonlight intruded through the windows thanks to the scudding clouds. But the glowing green facia of his mobile gave him a little more illumination, and it was this that led him to the door which previously had been locked but now stood open a couple of inches. Keith halted, bewildered. It was difficult to be sure whether or not the cavalry music had sounded from behind this, because Geoff's phone had now gone to voicemail. Irritably, Keith re-keyed the number, all the time wondering how any of this was possible. This door had definitely been locked earlier on.

But could someone have been waiting on the other side?

The *Garry Owen* sounded a second time. There was no doubt – it came from just beyond the open door. Keith's scalp twitched as he stood there. With hesitant footfalls, the two women ventured up the stairs behind him. Gruffly, he told them to go back down. Then almost barked with laughter. Why had he done that? Was he such a he-man that two women would only get in the way as he sorted out the bad guys? The idea was preposterous – he couldn't remember the last time he'd had a fight; probably at school, and he'd probably lost. But it was too late now. Sally and Rula hadn't gone back down, but they weren't coming any further up either.

Slowly, he pushed the door all the way open.

The sight of a steep, narrow, wooden flight of stairs unnerved him even more. The bare walls on either side of it were at least as viciously claw-marked as the landing. What paper was left hung in ribbon-like shreds. He ascended anyway, nostrils wrinkling at a faint, vaguely rancid aroma, cringing at each creaking footfall. He held his phone steadily in front to light the way, though within a few steps he could see right to the top, where a doorframe without a door beckoned to him.

Again, the quickstep of the *Garry Owen* cut out as the call went to voicemail.

'Geoff?' Keith said, though he said it so quietly – his mouth was so dry that he could barely form words – that it was highly likely nobody would hear him. Not that this mattered. He felt certain that if anyone was up there, they'd already know he was here. 'Geoff … you in trouble, mate?' He risked raising his voice as he ascended. 'Look … you and Rula can sort this out. It's not the problem you think it is.'

There was a faint rustling sound, like coarse fabric trailing across floorboards. Keith halted, ears straining. The rustling ceased. A hollow silence followed.

He glanced around. He'd passed half way now, but the staircase behind was a tilting shaft, the door at the bottom a dim oblong. He turned back to the upper door.

'Okay,' he said under his breath. Then, louder: 'Geoff, I'm coming up.'

He proceeded with hefty, clumping steps, determined to drown out any further sounds he might not want to hear. Part of the room above had now swum into view. He could make out a section of ceiling: more damp, scabrous plaster, but slanted. An attic.

He kept going. Only three stair-treads remained.

The rest of the room emerged through the narrow

doorway.

Like all the others, it was empty, gutted, bits of debris littering its bare floorboards, though there was some kind of upright shape at the far end, about twenty yards ahead of him. The aroma he'd noticed was now a nauseating stench. Keith stuck a finger under his nose as he edged forward, blinking as he tried to work out what he was seeing. Gradually it became clear. A curtain, on a free-standing rail – the sort of thing you saw in a hospital emergency bay. Its material was dingy, mildewed, the metal of its frame mottled with rust. There was a loud electronic *bleep* from the other side of it as Geoff's voicemail switched itself off.

Another rustling sound followed, this one protracted.

'Geoff?' Keith's voice had deadened to a whisper.

His left foot clouted some heavy object, and it rolled away. He risked a glance: it was long, thin and curved, with an ivory texture. Bone. That seemed so in keeping with the atmosphere in here, but he didn't dare look further for fear he'd see others just like it. Maybe many others, strewn amid the heaps of what he'd initially thought were rags, but now that his eyes had attuned, he could identify as black feathers. And there was no doubt about the stench, which was foetid beyond belief; it bespoke an animal pen of some sort ... or maybe a giant birdcage.

The rustling beyond the curtain ceased.

Keith was now only five yards from it, but his entire world had shrunk to that hanging square of filthy cloth. He was barely aware of himself as he shuffled the final distance. Breathless, he reached a gloved hand towards the edge of it. Another very brief rustling partially halted him, but then, with nerves so taut he thought they'd snap, he threw caution to the wind and lunged, snatching the material, tearing it back – to reveal another six or seven yards of attic space, empty except for additional piles of black feathers intermingled with bones and other carrion, and on top of it all, the distinctive shape of Geoff's iPhone.

Still holding his breath, Keith ventured forward, hunkered down and grabbed it.

He turned it over in his hands, wondering what tell-tale signs it might display: blood, shiny new claw-marks? But there was nothing. He glanced around; in the wall directly facing him there was a low circular casement. No glass remained in it, but tendrils of ivy hung through, scraping and rustling on the floor as they shifted in the breeze.

Keith's spine still crawled as he retreated from this, before turning and hurriedly kicking his way back through the detritus – only to spy a recess in the far corner of the attic, just left of the door he'd come in through. About eight feet across and five deep, it wasn't entirely concealed in shadow, but at first he couldn't make out the enormous word inscribed on the wall at the back of it. He veered towards it, activating the strong light on Geoff's iPhone. It still took several seconds to work out what had been written there, and not just because the letters had been jaggedly gouged in the rotted wallpaper, but at first because they appeared to make no sense:

HRAFNSMERKI

Keith leaned forward, squinting. He was only an amateur folklorist, a part-time historian. But he knew enough about his chosen subject to finally recognise this as Old Norse. And to realise what it meant: *Land-Waster*.

The stench now was overpowering, eye-watering. Slowly, he became aware of movement directly above his head, and heard a low burbling noise, like liquid glugging in a non-human throat. Clamping his bottom lip between his teeth, he flicked off the light in his hand, turned stiffly – and sped for the doorway, lunging out through it and charging wildly down the attic stair.

The two women met him on the landing.

'We've gotta get out of here!' he stammered, wrapping arms around both of them, and driving them towards the top of the main stairway.

'What?' Sally said.

'Now, Sally, now!'

'But where's Geoff?' Rula asked.

'Never mind Geoff. *We've* gotta get out.'

They blundered down the stair together, a struggling knot, constantly on the verge of tripping. But at the bottom, the women resisted more strongly.

'*Where's Geoff?*' Rula demanded.

'I don't know, I don't,' Keith stuttered. 'But *we've* got to go!' There was a dull creak upstairs. Face bursting with sweat, Keith hustled them roughly through the network of downstairs rooms to the back door. The horrible idea struck him that it might be closed and barred, but it wasn't. It stood open, half-covered by ivy. He drove them through it forcefully.

'Keith, you're hurting my arm!' Sally complained.

They floundered out into the passage at the side of the house, in the midst of icy wind and whipping rain. The shock of this seemed to bring Keith to his senses. He hesitated, not sure what he was thinking – until he heard the clattering up on the roof, the frenzied scraping of tiles. Despite their protestations, he stumbled on, pushing them around onto the forecourt and across it – anything to get them away from that house, which he sensed rising behind them like some immense, malevolent shadow.

'Hell ... hellion,' he said under his breath, as he shoved them towards the main gate.

'Hellion?' Sally replied. Now she spoke with fear herself. She'd never seen her husband like this before. 'You mean that Raven Man thing ...?'

'But that's just a myth, isn't it!' Rula said. It was a plea rather than a question.

Keith didn't answer. With the sounds of further motion behind them, another heavy clattering, as if slates had detached from the roof – or something had – he drove them headlong to the gate, shouting hoarsely, swearing at them to get a move on.

This time they obeyed. The climbed the gate side by side, none of them looking back, and at the first opportunity swerved off the drive onto the moor. Keith wasn't initially sure whether they were on the right path, but he didn't care. He knew which way they had to go – across this vast, sodden expanse – and this they did. At first, once in open space, their flight was assisted by the wind. It blew from behind them, but with no sure footing and a darkness that was near all-encompassing, it still almost knocked them from their feet. And then the path curved, or the wind simply switched around – suddenly it was driving into their faces, pelting them front-on with rain.

At least it was rain, Keith thought as he stumbled along, and not hail. Some of the hailstones he'd seen earlier would have flattened corn. Even so, the turmoil around them was torture; it pounded them left to right, sent them staggering on wobbling legs. The screaming of the wind was fit to burst their eardrums, if that *was* the wind. More than once, Keith fancied something swooped past just above their heads; an enormous, black something which blotted out the moon. That cloth or canvas he'd seen caught around the spire, blowing all over the place in the gale. That had to be it. Hadn't he heard it flapping as it passed them by? His throat was now raw with shouting at the women to hurry. They wept and sobbed in response, the elements battering them as they hobbled through the maelstrom. The adrenaline this created fuelled their strenuous efforts. It overcame the face-numbing wind, the energy-sapping chill. But then Rula squawked in horror as she stumbled, Sally striking her from behind and sending her face-first into a trackside quagmire, plastering her head to toe with black, festering ooze.

Keith tugged on her anorak hood, trying to haul her to her feet.

'Keith!' she wailed. 'You're pulling it over my bloody head!'

Sally lurched back towards them, to assist. Once they were all on their feet, they forged on, gaining new heart from the roar of the beck somewhere ahead. A short time later, the squat, square outline of the derelict shed emerged on their right.

'Almost there,' Keith gasped, the heart drumming in his chest. He hawked out a wad of hot phlegm as he glanced behind them. The Priory was lost to view. They'd done it. They'd made it. 'Hurry!' he urged them still. 'Just a few more yards ...'

And then the shed exploded.

Or at least it exploded *open*.

Right alongside them.

Splinters flew everywhere, and the thing that came

out, arms spread wide, gave the most towering, terrifying shriek any of them had ever heard.

By pure instinct, the trio flinched away. In fact, Keith ducked, gibbering, shouting unintelligibly. They dispersed like skittles, sliding in all directions, darkness and rain filling their faces as they tottered and toppled.

Until the sound of raucous male laughter brought them back to reality.

It was Geoff.

Even as they slowly, disbelievingly drew back together, he remained doubled over in the shed's broken doorway, laughing so hard they thought he would choke. 'Oh my God ... you lot! That ... that couldn't have worked better if I'd planned it.'

The trio exchanged breathless, wild-eyed glances.

'What ... what the hell are you talking about?' Sally panted.

'Well, I *did* plan it of course. Most of it. Not you running down here like the clappers though.' Geoff half-choked with laughter again, swaggering out from the shed as the force of the wind and rain appeared to ebb. 'I came out here last night ... while "Miss Loyalty 2015" thought I was kipping in the car. Couldn't sleep, could I? I mean in the car for God's sake ... after everything that's been going on. I knew we'd be coming to Thurmond Priory today, so I thought I'd drive out and look it over beforehand. Incredible place, isn't it? But when I saw that burn on the wall, those claw-marks, and that attic full of bones and feathers ... well, I just knew I had to do a disappearing act on you half way through. Make like the Raven Man had nabbed me.' He shook his head, still chuckling. 'It wasn't even difficult. Soon as you went back downstairs, Keith, I unlocked the attic – I'd found the key still in its door last night and had it with me all through today. Then it was down the creeper and I was off.'

'Geoff ...' Keith said, dazed, 'this is *so* not funny.'

Geoff eyed him narrowly. 'Hey, mate ... maybe it wasn't supposed to be funny. Maybe it was something that just had to be done.'

'You mean as a punishment for me?' Rula said, sounding strained and tearful. 'But what about the others? Seriously, Geoff ... just because I'd upset you, you thought it was okay to terrorise Keith and Sally too?'

Geoff glanced at Keith again, and shrugged. 'Sorry, guys ... you were collaterals to a certain extent.'

'You child!' Rula spat.

'Look who's talking!' He laughed again, drawing a finger across the muddy front of her anorak as he circled her, and smearing it down her otherwise spotless back. 'Been making mud pies again, darling?'

'Oh, you're a real scream,' she retorted.

'Actually, this is a good look for you, Rula. One half dirty, the other clean. What was it you said about the hellion, Keith?'

Keith waved him away. 'Don't involve me in this, mate.'

'We're none of us all good, none of us all bad.' Geoff turned back to his wife. 'At least that's glaringly obvious where *you're* concerned.'

Sally now intervened, voice quaking with disgust. 'Geoffrey Wade, this is the stupidest thing that anyone I've ever known has ever done!'

'Yeah, but at least in the morning, Sal, you'll still have a happy life to go back to ... so I think you'll get over it.'

Too infuriated to respond further, Sally turned and

strode stiffly towards the beck. Rula went with her, neither of them looking back. Without a word, Keith handed Geoff his iPhone, and set off after them. Geoff pocketed the device as he brought up the rear, still sniggering to himself.

Keith wanted to berate him more forcefully, but perhaps for now the silent treatment was best – things got said in stressful moments that were often irretrievable, and it wasn't like Geoff wasn't already hurting deeply. Besides, Geoff's stupid trick had brought Keith back to the real world with a bang, and he was now more annoyed with himself. Firstly because, having cajoled the two women across the moor in a panic-stricken funk, he'd then caterwauled and jabbered at the first sight of actual danger, revealing with painful obviousness that he wasn't the cool hero most men liked to think they were. And secondly, deep down – and this was a *very* personal annoyance – because he'd not only given credit to the notion of the Raven Man, a daft fairy tale from long, long ago, he'd come to believe it so quickly and with such conviction that he'd actually imagined he'd seen the damn thing, that he'd run from it, madly, blindly. Anyone with half a brain should have realised what was going on back there: a stench of wet-rot, an old leaky pipe gurgling, those feathers and bones – any normal scavenger might have made its nest up there.

A shadow crossed the moon.

Keith didn't bother looking up. A piece of rag tossed on the wind? Another scudding raincloud? Who cared? He shook his head, vexed beyond belief that he'd descended so swiftly from his status as keeper of the mysterious to idiotic believer.

And it wasn't as if they didn't have real problems to

contend with. Just ahead, the women had reached the bridge, at which point they'd stopped, shocked. The beck was flowing *over* it. Only by a couple of inches, but the footway was actually submerged, the handrails to either side, which had felt rickety enough before, quivering violently with the impacts of the current.

'I don't think this is a very good idea,' Sally said tightly.

'Yeah, but ... well, we can't stay here,' Rula replied. 'We'll die from exposure.'

'And I'm not going back,' Keith said, glancing over his shoulder into the blackness. He might think himself a fool for giving credence to the crazy legend of Thurmond Priory, but he was damned if he was ever venturing back under its dank, decrepit roof.

'Jesus, you lot are pathetic,' Geoff said, shouldering his way through and starting across, though Keith noticed that his hands were clamped tightly to the rails. He progressed with heavy cautious footsteps, the river sloshing over his ankles, but he still turned round to look at them when he was half way. 'Come on, it's perfectly safe ... it can take all four of us at the same time, this!'

'I suggest we don't put *that* theory to the test,' Keith said quietly.

The women mumbled in agreement.

They all recognised this for what it was: a dash of reckless bravado from a guy who valued his 'outdoorsman' tag and as such was now trying to compensate for what he maybe realised had been a childish display a few minutes earlier. But at least it served a purpose; it would show how sturdy the bridge was.

A torturous *creak* sounded somewhere behind them.

THE HELLION

Keith glanced back again, this time towards the distant, sagging outline of the shed. From here it was only partially visible, but it didn't look any different. He supposed it could have shifted position in the wind. It was old, flimsy as Hell. Geoff bursting through its door could easily have caused structural damage.

Geoff meanwhile had made it to the other bank. He spun around with arms outspread, as if to indicate how easy it had been, and how perhaps how foolish they were to have expected otherwise. There was second curious sound from their rear, another prolonged wooden *creak*. Keith glanced again at the shed. It looked as it had before, except ...

As the clouds progressively cleared, his eyes were attuning to the intensifying moonlight. Even so, he had to squint. Was something perched on top of the shed? Something large and ungainly? Something that looked like ...?

Scalp prickling and lips tightening, he turned back to the river.

'Time for us to go!' he said simply.

Sally stumbled towards the bridge, propelled by her husband's unsympathetic hand. 'Keith!'

There was a snap of annoyance in her voice, but knowing she had no choice, she went.

'You too, Rula,' Keith pushed the second woman forward.

'Both at the same time?' Rula said, surprised and not a little scared.

'What's up, Rula!' Geoff called mockingly from the far shore. 'Do you only take chances these days if there's something a bit naughty in it for you?'

Rula didn't reply to that; she was too unnerved by the prospect in front of her. However, Keith continued edging her forward, assuring her that they *had* to get going.

She finally did as he said, shuffling out in pursuit of Sally, who was now at half way. Keith threw another glance over his shoulder. There was nothing at all on the shed roof. He blinked hard, squinted again. Still nothing. But he took no comfort from this, especially as a third weird sound now assailed them. Not wood, this time – how could it be that when it came from far overhead? A screech of some sort?

Sally was almost at the other side. But Rula, moving more cautiously, whimpering as she went, still hadn't reached half way.

Yet another shadow wheeled across the moon.

Keith marched forward. The bridge, already shuddering, shook violently beneath his weight. Both Sally and Rula looked back. The latter's face was written with terror, but Keith pressed on, hand-pulling himself forwards, plunging with each step to a depth of half his shins.

'Keep going!' he shouted.

'Keith ... no!' Rula protested. 'You can't come yet ... this thing'll collapse!'

'Just keep going!'

Absurdly, she started making her way back towards him.

'Rula, what are you doing?'

Geoff bellowed with laughter as he watched.

'It's going to collapse!' she wailed. 'I know it is!'

'You stupid bloody woman!' Keith roared.

Another screech, descending fast towards them.

Rula had almost got back to him, but he couldn't step aside. Instead, he stopped rigid, blocking her path. His eyes met hers, but she didn't understand. *He* was

THE HELLION

the one it wanted, *he* was the one who'd brought them here. This had been *his* plan ... even if it was plain to all that *she* deserved it most. He dropped to his knees, arms wrapped around his head, squashing himself into a ball as the river foamed up his back.

And it took Rula instead.

The immense, stinking, spread-eagled thing, all bony claws, stretched membrane and black tarry feathers – though he sensed it rather than saw it as it swooped over him with inches to spare, buffeting him with the force of its passage.

The woman screamed hoarsely as she ascended rapidly from view.

There were two seconds of stunned silence before Geoff responded.

'What the fuck!' he howled, charging forward, barging past Sally and clomping along the flooded footway with his heavy feet.

'Geoff, for God's sake!' Sally tried to grapple with him. He failed to shake her off, and so dragged her with him.

'What the fuck, Keith! What the ... what the fuck just happened? Where's Rula?'

Keith couldn't answer immediately. He used the handrail to drag himself to his feet, swaying with the sickness, despair and dizziness of it all.

At least he *thought* that was why he was swaying.

Another shriek assailed them, a shrill, piercing ululation from high overhead. It bespoke horror, agony, and came down amid a fresh, heavy shower – which they might have mistaken for rain had it not been so warm.

Sally herself screamed. Geoff sobbed his wife's name.

Keith closed his eyes, his world no longer swaying but turning over completely as the bridge supports gave, the entire structure tipping, casting them all together into the boiling, foaming flood.

Thurmond Priory, a derelict Victorian house, still stands in a shallow vale on the North York Moors, at the end of a stony road that leads nowhere else. With its past a mystery and its ownership in seemingly permanent dispute, it is a picture of melancholy, an image of forlorn isolation. But it is a scenic spot, this, especially when the sky is blue, and the sun shines, and the rich green carpet of encircling grassland glimmers gold with asphodel or purple/pink with August heather. It would make an ideal summer home, especially for those seeking peace, solitude, a return to nature. It needs refurbishment, of course: the roof, the windows, the teetering, misaligned chimneys; the interior too should be gutted and restored. But there is much about Thurmond Priory to like – the stillness that wreathes it, its air of faded antiquity – and if from a distance one sees a dark and shapeless thing apparently clinging to the spire of its central-most tower, one needn't be concerned. A piece of windblown cloth no doubt, an errant canvas, black with damp and rot, caught in the timeless moorland wind

About The Author

Paul Finch is a former cop and journalist, and, having read History at Goldsmiths College, London, a qualified historian, though he currently earns his living as a full-time writer.

He cut his literary teeth penning episodes of the British TV crime drama, *The Bill*, and has written extensively in the field of children's animation. However, he is probably best known for his work in thrillers, dark fantasy and horror, in which capacity he is a two-time winner of the British Fantasy Award and a one-time winner of the International Horror Guild Award.

He is responsible for numerous short stories and novellas, but also for two horror movies (a third of his, *War Wolf*, is in pre-production), and for a series of best-selling crime novels featuring the British police detective, Mark 'Heck' Heckenburg.

Paul lives in Lancashire, UK, with his wife Cathy and his children, Eleanor and Harry. His website can be found at http://paulfinch-writer.blogspot.co.uk/ and he can be followed on Twitter as @paulfinchauthor.

Of *Cape Wrath*, he says: 'It sprang purely from my love of British history, in particular the darker, wilder periods before the developments of science and reason. There are certain places in the more remote parts of the British Isles where it is easy to imagine yourself back in those far-off, lawless days, and Cape Wrath – which, for anyone who doesn't know, is a real location – is certainly one of them.

'Of course, ancient and medieval history is not just about murder and destruction, but in our cosseted world of the 21st century it's nearly impossible to imagine just how brutal and frightening everyday life must have been in that lost era. *Cape Wrath* is a horror story with a contemporary setting, but if anyone who reads it is reminded, even for a second, that the ground they tread daily is the same ground once trodden by warlike barbarous hordes, then I'll consider it a job well done.'

ALSO AVAILABLE FROM TELOS PUBLISHING

HORROR/FANTASY

DAVID J HOWE
TALESPINNING

URBAN GOTHIC: LACUNA AND OTHER TRIPS
edited by DAVID J HOWE

SAM STONE
THE JINX CHRONICLES
1: JINX TOWN
2: JINX MAGIC (Autumn 2015)
3: JINX BOUND (Autumn 2016)

KAT LIGHTFOOT MYSTERIES
1: ZOMBIES AT TIFFANY'S
2: KAT ON A HOT TIN AIRSHIP
3: WHAT'S DEAD PUSSYKAT
4: KAT OF GREEN TENTACLES (Autumn 2015)

THE DARKNESS WITHIN: FINAL CUT

ZOMBIES IN NEW YORK AND OTHER BLOODY JOTTINGS

RAVEN DANE
DEATH'S DARK WINGS
ABSINTHE & ARSENIC

SHROUDED BY DARKNESS: TALES OF TERROR
edited by ALISON L R DAVIES
An anthology of tales guaranteed to bring a chill to the spine. This collection has been published to raise money for DebRA, a national charity working on behalf of people with the genetic skin blistering condition, Epidermolysis Bullosa (EB). Featuring stories by: Debbie Bennett, Poppy Z Brite, Simon Clark, Storm Constantine, Peter Crowther, Alison L R Davies, Paul Finch, Christopher Fowler, Neil Gaiman, Gary Greenwood, David J Howe, Dawn Knox, Tim Lebbon, Charles de Lint, Steven Lockley & Paul Lewis, James Lovegrove, Graham Masterton, Richard Christian Matheson, Justina Robson, Mark Samuels, Darren Shan and Michael Marshall Smith. With a frontispiece by Clive Barker and a foreword by Stephen Jones. Deluxe hardback cover by Simon Marsden.

HELEN MCCABE
THE PIPER TRILOGY
PIPER
THE PIERCING
CODEX (Autumn 2015)

SIMON CLARK
HUMPTY'S BONES
THE FALL

GRAHAM MASTERTON
RULES OF DUEL
THE DJINN

KING OF ALL THE DEAD by STEVE LOCKLEY & PAUL LEWIS

THE HUMAN ABSTRACT by GEORGE MANN

BREATHE by CHRISTOPHER FOWLER
The Office meets *Night of the Living Dead.*

HOUDINI'S LAST ILLUSION by STEVE SAVILE

ALICE'S JOURNEY BEYOND THE MOON by R J CARTER

APPROACHING OMEGA by ERIC BROWN

VALLEY OF LIGHTS by STEPHEN GALLAGHER

PRETTY YOUNG THINGS by DOMINIC MCDONAGH

A MANHATTAN GHOST STORY by T M WRIGHT

FORCE MAJEURE by DANIEL O'MAHONY

BLACK TIDE by DEL STONE JR

DOCTOR TRIPPS: KAIJU COCKTAIL by KIT COX

SPECTRE by STEPHEN LAWS

CAPTAINS STUPENDOUS by RHYS HUGHES

TELOS PUBLISHING
Email: orders@telos.co.uk
Web: www.telos.co.uk

To order copies of any Telos books, please visit our website where there are full details of all titles and facilities for worldwide credit card online ordering, as well as occasional special offers.

Printed in Great Britain
by Amazon.co.uk, Ltd.,
Marston Gate.